Enid Blyton's
THE ENCHANTED
WOOD

The children looked up into the broad, leafy boughs of the tree. They felt tremendously excited. The Faraway Tree in the Enchanted Wood! Oh, what magic there seemed to be in the very names!

They picked up their basket and went home, all of them thinking the same thought:

"We *must* go up the Faraway Tree and see what is at the top!"

Enid Blyton's

THE ENCHANTED
WOOD

mammoth

First published in Great Britain 1939 by Newnes
Published 1991 by Mammoth
This edition first published 1999 by Mammoth
an imprint of Egmont Children's Books Limited
239 Kensington High Street, London W8 6SA

Text copyright © Enid Blyton Limited

Copyright in original stories and characters Enid Blyton Limited
Audio-visual series copyright Abbey Home Entertainment Limited 1997
Enid Blyton's signature is a Registered Trade Mark of
Enid Blyton Limited

ISBN 0 7497 3209 1

21 23 25 27 29 30 28 28 26 24 22

A CIP catalogue record for this title
is available from the British Library

Printed in Great Britain
by Cox & Wyman Ltd, Reading, Berkshire

CONTENTS

I

HOW THEY FOUND THE MAGIC WOOD

There were once three children, called Jo, Bessie, and Fanny. All their lives they had lived in a town, but now their father had a job in the country, so they were all to move as soon as ever they could.

"What fun to be in the country!" said Jo. "I shall learn all about animals and birds!"

"And I shall pick as many flowers as I want to," said Bessie.

"And I shall have a garden of my own," said Fanny.

When the day came for the move all the children were excited. A small van came to their door and two men helped their father and mother to pile everything into it. When it was full the van drove away, and the children put on their coats and hats to go with their father and mother to catch a train at the station.

"Now we're off!" cried Jo.

"The country, the country!" sang Bessie.

"We might see fairies there!" said Fanny.

The train whistled, and chuffed out of the station. The children pressed their noses to the window and watched the dirty houses and the tall chimneys race by. How they hated the town! How lovely it would be to be in the clean country, with flowers growing everywhere, and birds singing in the hedges!

"We might have adventures in the country," said Jo. "There will be streams and hillsides, big fields and dark woods. Oooh, it will be lovely!"

"You won't have any more adventures in the country than you will have in the town," said their father. "I dare say you will find it all very dull."

But that's where he was quite wrong. My goodness, the things that happened to those three children!

They arrived at last at the tiny station where they were to get out. A sleepy-looking porter put their two bags on a barrow, and said he would bring them along later. Off they all went down the winding country lane, chattering loudly.

"I wonder what our cottage will be like?" said Bessie.

"And I wonder if we've got a garden?" said Fanny.

But long before they reached their new home they were tired out and could not bother to say a word more to each other. Their cottage was five miles from the station, and as the children's father could not afford to do anything but walk there, it seemed a very long way indeed. There was no bus to take them, so the tired children dragged their feet along, wishing for a cup of milk and a cosy bed.

At last they got there—and dear me, it was worth all the walk, for the cottage was sweet. Roses hung from the walls—red and white and pink—and honeysuckle was all round the front door. It was lovely!

The van was at the door, and the two men were moving all the furniture into the little house. Father helped, whilst Mother went to light the kitchen fire to make them all a hot drink.

They were so tired that they could do nothing but drink hot milk, eat a few biscuits, and tumble into their roughly-made beds. Jo looked out of the window but he was too sleepy to see properly. In one minute the two girls in their small room were asleep, and Jo too, in his even tinier room.

What fun it was to wake up in the morning and see the sun shining in at strange windows! It didn't take Jo, Bessie, and Fanny very long to dress. Then they were out in the little garden, running through the grass that had grown so long, and smelling the roses that grew all around.

Mother cooked eggs for them, and they ate their breakfast hungrily.

"It's lovely to be in the country!" said Jo, looking out of the window to the far-away hills.

"We can grow vegetables in the garden," said Bessie.

"There will be glorious walks all round," said Fanny.

That day every one helped to get the little house straight and tidy. Father was going to work the next day. Mother hoped there would be some one to give her washing to do, then she would make enough money to buy a few hens. That would be lovely!

"I shall collect the eggs each morning and evening," said Fanny happily.

"Let's go out and see what the country round about is like," said Jo. "Can you spare us for an hour, Mother?"

"Yes, run along," said Mother. So off the three children went, out of the tiny white front gate and into the lane.

They explored all round about. They ran across a field where pink clover was full of bees. They paddled in a small brown stream that chattered away to itself under the willow trees in the sunshine.

And then they suddenly came to the wood. It was not far from their cottage, at the back. It looked quite an ordinary wood, except that the trees were a darker green than usual. A narrow ditch separated the wood from the overgrown lane.

"A wood!" said Bessie, in delight. "We shall be able to have picnics here!"

"It's rather a mysterious sort of wood," said Jo thoughtfully. "Don't you think so, Bessie?"

"Well, the trees are rather thick, but they seem about the same as any others," said Bessie.

"They don't quite," said Fanny. "The noise the leaves make is different. Listen!"

They listened—and Fanny was right. The leaves of the trees in the wood did not rustle in quite the same way as other trees nearby did.

"It's almost as if they were really talking to one another," said Bessie. "Whispering secrets—real secrets, that we just can't understand."

"It's a magic wood!" said Fanny suddenly.

Nobody said anything. They stood and listened. "Wisha-wisha-wisha-wisha-wisha!" said the trees in the wood, and bent towards one another in a friendly way.

"There might be fairy-folk in there," said Bessie. "Shall we jump over the ditch and go in?"

"No," said Jo. "We might get lost. Let's find our way around before we go into big woods like this."

"Jo! Bessie! Fanny!" suddenly came their mother's voice from the cottage not far off. "Tea-time, tea-time!"

The children felt hungry all at once. They forgot the queer wood and ran back to their new home. Mother had new bread with strawberry jam for

9

them, and they ate a whole loaf between them.

Father came in as they were finishing. He had been shopping for Mother in the village three miles away and he was hungry and tired.

"We've been exploring everywhere, Father," said Bessie, pouring him out a big cup of tea.

"We've found a lovely wood," said Fanny.

"It's a queer sort of wood," said Jo. "The trees really seem to be talking to one another, Father."

"That must be the wood I've heard about this afternoon," said Father. "It has a strange name, children."

"What is it called?" asked Jo.

"It's called the Enchanted Wood," said their father. "People don't go there if they can help it. It's funny to hear things like this nowadays, and I don't expect there is really anything very queer about the wood. But just be careful not to go too far into it, in case you get lost."

The children looked in excitement at one another. The Enchanted Wood! What a lovely name!

And each child secretly thought the same thought—"I shall go and explore the Enchanted Wood as soon as ever I can!"

Their father set them to work in the overgrown garden after tea. Jo had to pull up the tough thistles and the two girls had to weed the untidy vegetable bed. They spoke to one another in joyful voices.

"The Enchanted Wood! We knew there was something queer about it!"

"I guessed there were fairies there!" said Fanny.

"We'll do some more exploring as soon as we can!" cried Bessie. "We'll find out what those whispering trees are saying! We'll know all the secrets of the wood before many weeks are past!"

And that night, at bedtime, all three stood at the window, looking out on the dark, whispering wood behind the cottage. What would they find in the Enchanted Wood?

II

FIRST VISIT TO THE WOOD

The three children had no chance to visit the Enchanted Wood until the next week, because they had to help their mother and father all they could. There was the garden to get tidy, curtains to sew for the house, and a great deal of cleaning to be done.

Sometimes Jo was free and could have gone by himself. Sometimes the girls were sent out for a walk, but Jo was busy. None of them wanted to go without the others, so they had to wait. And then at last their chance came.

"You can take your tea out to-day," said Mother. "You've worked well, all of you, and you deserve a picnic. I'll cut you some sandwiches, and you can take a bottle of milk."

"We'll go to the Wood!" whispered Bessie to the others, and with excited faces and beating hearts they helped their mother to pack their tea into a big basket.

They set off. There was a small gate at the bottom of their back garden that led into the overgrown lane running by the wood. They unlatched the gate and stood in the lane. They could see the trees in the wood, and hear them talking their strange tree-talk: "Wisha-wisha-wisha-wisha!"

"I feel as if there are adventures about," said Jo. "Come on! Over the ditch we go—and into the Enchanted Wood!"

One by one the children jumped over the narrow ditch. They stood beneath the trees and peered about. Small freckles of sunshine lay here and there on the ground, but not very many, for the trees were so thick. It was dim and green there, and a small bird nearby sang a queer little song over and over again.

"It really *is* magic!" said Fanny suddenly. "I can feel magic about somewhere, can't you, Bessie? Can't you, Jo?"

"Yes," said the others, and their eyes shone with excitement. "Come on!"

They went down a little green path that looked as if it had been made for rabbits, it was so small and narrow.

"Don't let's go too far," said Jo. "We had better wait till we know the paths a bit better before we go deep into the wood. Look about for a good place to sit down and have our sandwiches, girls."

"I can see some wild strawberries!" cried Bessie, and she knelt down and pressed back some pretty leaves, showing the others deep red strawberries below.

"Let's pick some and have them for tea too," said Fanny. So they picked hard, and soon had enough to make a fine meal.

"Let's sit down under that old oak tree over there," said Jo. "It's all soft moss beneath. It will be like sitting on a green velvet cushion."

So they sat down, and undid their sandwiches. Soon they were munching away happily, listening to the dark green leaves overhead saying "Wisha-wisha" all the time.

And it was whilst they were in the middle of their tea that they saw a very peculiar thing. Fanny noticed it first.

Not far off was a clear piece of soft grass. As Fanny looked at it she noticed bumps appearing on it. She stared in surprise. The bumps grew. The earth rose up and broke in about six places.

"Look!" said Fanny, in a low voice, pointing to the piece of grass. "What's happening over there?"

All three watched in silence. And then they saw what it was. Six big toadstools were growing quickly up from the ground, pushing their way through, and rising up steadily!

"I've never seen *that* happen before!" said Jo, in astonishment.

"Sh!" said Bessie. "Don't make a noise. I can hear footsteps."

The others listened. Sure enough they heard the sound of pattering feet and little high voices.

"Let's get quickly behind a bush," said Bessie suddenly. "Whoever it is that is coming will be frightened if they see us. There's magic happening here, and we want to see it!"

They scrambled up and crept quietly behind a thick bush, taking their basket with them. They hid just in time, for even as Bessie settled down and parted the leaves of the bush to peep through, there came a troop of small men with long beards almost reaching the ground!

"Brownies!" whispered Jo.

The brownies went to the toadstools and sat down on them. They were holding a meeting. One of them had a bag with him which he put down behind his toadstool. The children could not hear what was being said, but they heard the sound of the chattering voices, and caught one or two words.

Suddenly Jo nudged Bessie and Fanny. He had seen something else. The girls saw it too. An ugly, gnome-like fellow was creeping up silently behind the meeting on the toadstools. None of the brownies saw him or heard him.

"He's after that bag!" whispered Jo. And so he was! He reached out a long arm. His bony fingers closed on the bag. He began to draw it away under a bush.

Jo jumped up. He was not going to watch people being robbed without saying something! He shouted loudly:

"Stop thief! Hi, look at that gnome behind you!"

In a fright the brownies all leapt up. The gnome jumped to his feet and sped off with the bag. The brownies stared after him in dismay, not one of them following him. The robber ran towards the children's bush. He didn't know they were there.

As quick as lightning Jo put out his foot and tripped up the running gnome. Down he went, crash! The bag flew from his hand and Bessie picked it up and threw it to the astonished brownies, who were still standing by the toadstools. Jo tried to grab the gnome—but he was up and off like a bird.

The children tore after him. In between the

trees they went, dodging here and there — and at last they saw the gnome leap up to the low branches of a great tree, and pull himself into the leaves. The children sank down at the bottom, out of breath.

"We've got him now!" said Jo. "He can't get down without being caught!"

"Here are the brownies coming," said Bessie, wiping her hot forehead. The little bearded men ran up and bowed.

"You are very good to us," said the biggest one. "Thank you for saving our bag. We have valuable papers in there."

"We've got the gnome for you too," said Jo, as he pointed up into the tree. "He went up there. If you surround the tree and wait, you will be able to catch him as he comes down."

But the brownies would not come too near the tree. They looked half frightened of it.

"He will not come down until he wants to," said the biggest brownie. "That is the oldest and most magic tree in the world. It is the Faraway Tree."

"The Faraway Tree!" said Bessie, in wonder "What a queer name! Why do you call it that?"

"It's a very strange tree," said another brownie. "Its top reaches the far-away places in a way we don't understand. Sometimes its top branches may be in Witchland, sometimes in lovely countries, sometimes in peculiar places that no one has ever heard of. We never climb it because we never know what might be at the top!"

"How very strange!" said the children.

"The gnome has got into whatever place there is at the top of the tree to-day," said the biggest brownie. "He may live there for months and never come down again. It's no good waiting for him—and it's certainly no good going after him. His name is Creepy, because he is for ever creeping about quietly."

The children looked up into the broad, leafy boughs of the tree. They felt tremendously excited. The Faraway Tree in the Enchanted Wood! Oh, what magic there seemed to be in the very names!

"If only we could climb up!" said Jo longingly.

"You must never do that," said the brownies, at once. "It's dangerous. We must go now—but we do thank you for your help. If ever you want us to help *you*, just come into the Enchanted Wood and whistle seven times under the oak tree not far from our toadstools."

"Thank you," said the children, and stared after the six small brownies as they ran off between the trees. Jo thought it was time to go home, so they followed the little men down the narrow green path until they came to the part of the wood they knew. They picked up their basket and went home, all of them thinking the same thought:

"We *must* go up the Faraway Tree and see what is at the top!"

III

UP THE FARAWAY TREE

The children did not tell their father and mother about the happenings in the Enchanted Wood, for they were so afraid that they might be forbidden to go there. But when they were alone they talked about nothing else.

"When do you suppose we could go up the Faraway Tree?" Fanny kept asking. "Oh, do let's go, Jo."

Jo wanted to go very badly — but he was a little afraid of what might happen, and he knew that he ought to look after his two sisters and see that no harm ever came to them. Just suppose they all went up the Faraway Tree and never came back!

Then he had an idea. "Listen," he said. "I know what we'll do? We'll climb up the tree and just *see* what is at the top! We don't need to go there — we can just look. We'll wait till we have a whole day to ourselves, then we'll go."

The girls were so excited. They worked hard in the house hoping that their mother would say they could have a whole day to themselves. Jo worked hard in the garden, too, clearing away all the weeds. Their parents were very pleased.

"Would you like to go to the nearest town and have a day there?" asked Mother, at last.

"No, thank you," said Jo, at once. "We've had enough of towns, Mother! What we'd really like is to go and have a whole-day picnic in the wood!"

"Very well," said Mother. "You can go to-morrow. Father and I are going off for the day to buy some things we need. You can take your dinner and tea and go off by yourselves, if it is fine and sunny."

How the children hoped the day would be fine! They woke early and jumped out of bed. They pulled their curtains and looked out. The sky was as blue as cornflowers. The sun shone between the trees, and the shadows lay long and dewy on the grass. The Enchanted Wood stood dark and mysterious behind their garden.

They all had breakfast, then Mother cut sandwiches, put cakes into a bag, and three biscuits each. She sent Jo to pick some plums from the garden, and told Bessie to take two bottles of lemonade. The children were most excited.

Mother and Father set off to the town. The children waved good-bye from the gate. Then they tore indoors to get the bag in which their food had been put. They slammed the cottage door. Ah, adventures were in the air that morning!

> "Up the Faraway Tree,
> Jo, Bessie, and Me!"

sang Fanny loudly.

"Hush!" said Jo. "We are not far from the Enchanted Wood. We don't want any one to know what we're going to do."

They ran down the back garden and out of the

little gate at the end. They stood still in the overgrown, narrow lane and looked at one another. It was the first big adventure of their lives! What were they going to see? What were they going to do?

They jumped over the ditch into the wood. At once they felt different. Magic was round them. The birds' songs sounded different. The trees once again whispered secretly to one another: "Wisha-wisha-wisha-wisha!"

"Ooooh!" said Fanny, shivering with delight.

"Come on," said Jo, going down the green path. "Let's find the Faraway Tree."

They followed him. He went on till he came to the oak tree under which they had sat before. There were the six toadstools too, on which the brownies had held their meeting, though the toadstools looked rather brown and old now.

"Which is the way now?" said Bessie, stopping.

None of them knew. They set off down a little path, but they soon stopped, for they came to a strange place where the trees stood so close together that they could go no farther. They went back to the oak tree.

"Let's go this other way," said Bessie, so they set off in a different direction. But this time they came to a curious pond, whose waters were pale yellow, and shone like butter. Bessie didn't like the look of the pond at all, and they all three went back once more to the oak tree.

"This is too bad," said Fanny, almost crying. "Just when we've got a whole day to ourselves we

20

can't find the tree!"

"I'll tell you what we'll do," said Jo suddenly. "We'll call those brownies. Don't you remember how they said they would help us whenever we wanted them?"

"Of course!" said Fanny. "We had to stand under this oak tree and whistle seven times!"

"Go on, Jo, whistle," said Bessie. So Jo stood beneath the thick green leaves of the old oak and whistled loudly, seven times — "Phooee, phooee, phooee, phooee, phooee, phooee, phooee!"

The children waited. In about half a minute a rabbit popped its head out of a nearby rabbit-hole and stared at them.

"Who do you want?" said the rabbit, in a furry sort of voice.

The children stared in surprise. They had never heard an animal speak before. The rabbit put its ears up and down and spoke again, rather crossly.

"Are you deaf? Who do you WANT? I said."

"We want one of the brownies," said Jo, finding his tongue at last.

The rabbit turned and called down his hole, "Mr. Whiskers! Mr. Whiskers! There's some one wanting you!"

There came a voice shouting something in answer, and then one of the six brownies squeezed out of the rabbit-hole and stared at the children.

"Sorry to be so long," he said. "One of the rabbit's children has the measles, and I was down seeing to it."

"I didn't think rabbits got the measles," said Bessie, astonished.

"They more often get the weasels," said Mr. Whiskers. "Weasels are even more catching than measles, as far as rabbits are concerned."

He grinned as if he had made a huge joke, but as the children had no idea that weasels were savage little animals that caught rabbits, they didn't laugh.

"We wanted to ask you the way to the Faraway Tree," said Bessie. "We've forgotten it."

"I'll take you," said Mr. Whiskers, whose name was really a very good one, for his beard reached his toes. Sometimes he trod on it, and this jerked his head downwards suddenly. Bessie kept wanting to laugh but she thought she had better not. She wondered why he didn't tie it round his waist out of the way of his feet.

Mr. Whiskers led the way between the dark trees. At last he reached the trunk of the enormous Faraway Tree. "Here you are!" he said. "Are you expecting some one down it to-day?"

"Well, no," said Jo. "We rather wanted to go up it ourselves."

"Go up it yourselves!" said Mr. Whiskers, in horror. "Don't be silly. It's dangerous. You don't know what might be at the top. There's a different place almost every day!"

"Well, we're going," said Jo firmly, and he set his foot against the trunk of the tremendous tree and took hold of a branch above his head. "Come on, girls!"

"I shall fetch my brothers and get you down," said Mr. Whiskers, in a fright, and he scuttled off, crying, "It's so dangerous! It's so dangerous!"

"Do you suppose it *is* all right to go?" asked Bessie, who was usually the sensible one.

"Come on, Bessie!" said Jo impatiently. "We're only going to *see* what's at the top! Don't be a baby!"

"I'm not," said Bessie, and she and Fanny hauled themselves up beside Jo. "It doesn't look *very* difficult to climb. We'll soon be at the top."

But it wasn't as easy as they thought, as you will see!

IV

THE FOLK IN THE FARAWAY TREE

Before very long the children were hidden in the branches as they climbed upwards. When Mr. Whiskers came back with five other brownies, not a child could be seen!

"Hie, come down!" yelled the brownies, dancing round the tree. "You'll be captured or lost. This tree is dangerous!"

Jo laughed and peered down. The Faraway Tree seemed to be growing acorns just where he was, so he picked one and threw it down. It hit Mr. Whiskers on the hat and he rushed away, shouting, "Oh, some one's shot me! Some one's shot me!"

Then there was silence. "They've gone," said Jo, laughing again. "I expect they're afraid of being shot by acorn bullets, funny little things! Come on, girls!"

"This must be an oak tree if it grows acorns," said Bessie, as she climbed. But just as she said that she stared in surprise at something nearby. It was a prickly chestnut case, with conkers inside!

"Good gracious!" she said. "It's growing horse chestnuts just here! What a very peculiar tree!"

"Well, let's hope it will grow apples and pears higher up," said Fanny, with a giggle. "It's a most extraordinary tree!"

Soon they were quite high up. When Jo parted

the leaves and tried to see out of the tree he was amazed to find that he was far higher than the tallest trees in the wood. He and the girls looked down on the top of all the other trees, which looked like a broad green carpet below.

Jo was higher up than the girls. Suddenly he gave a shout. "I say, girls! Come up here by me, quickly! I've found something queer!"

Bessie and Fanny climbed quickly up.

"Why, it's a window in the tree!" said Bessie, in astonishment. They all peered inside, and suddenly the window was flung open and an angry little face looked out, with a nightcap on.

"Rude creatures!" shouted the angry little man, who looked like a pixie. "Everybody that climbs the tree peeps in at me! It doesn't matter what I'm doing, there's always some one peeping!"

The children were too astonished to do anything but stare. The pixie disappeared and came back with a jug of water. He flung it at Bessie and wetted her. She gave a scream.

"Perhaps you won't peep into people's houses next time," said the pixie with a grin, and he slammed his window shut again and drew the curtain.

"Well!" said Bessie, trying to wipe herself dry with her handkerchief. "What a rude little man!"

"We'd better not look in at any windows we pass," said Jo. "But I was so surprised to *see* a window in the tree!"

Bessie soon got dry. They climbed up again, and soon had another surprise. They came to a broad branch that led to a yellow door set neatly in the big trunk of the Faraway Tree. It had a little knocker and a brightly polished bell. The children stared at the door.

"I wonder who lives there?" said Fanny.

"Shall we knock and see?" said Jo.

"Well, I don't want water all over me again," said Bessie.

"We'll ring the bell and then hide behind this branch," said Jo. "If any one thinks he is going to throw water at us he won't find us."

So Jo rang the bell and then they all hid carefully behind a big branch. A voice came from the inside of the door.

"I'm washing my hair! If that's the butcher, please leave a pound of sausages!"

The children stared at one another and laughed. It was odd to hear of butchers coming up the Faraway Tree. The voice shouted again:

"If it's the oil man, I don't want anything. If it's the red dragon, he must call again next week!"

"Good gracious!" said Bessie, looking rather frightened. "The red dragon! I don't like the sound of that!"

At that moment the yellow door opened and a small elf looked out. Her hair was fluffed out round her shoulders, drying, and she was rubbing it with a towel. She stared at the peeping children.

"Did *you* ring my bell?" she asked. "What do you want?"

"We just wanted to see who lived in the funny

little tree-house," said Jo, peering in at the dark room inside the tree. The elf smiled. She had a very sweet face.

"Come in for a moment," she said. "My name is Silky, because of my silky hair. Where are you off to?"

"We are climbing up the Faraway Tree to see what is at the top," said Jo.

"Be careful you don't find something horrid," said Silky, giving them each a chair in her dark little tree-room. "Sometimes there are delightful places at the top of the tree—but sometimes there are queer lands too. Last week there was the land of Hippetty-Hop, which was dreadful. As soon as you got there, you had to hop on one leg, and everything went hippetty-hop, even the trees. Nothing ever kept still. It was most tiring."

"It does sound exciting," said Bessie. "Where's our food, Jo? Let's ask Silky to have some."

Silky was pleased. She sat there brushing her beautiful golden hair and ate sandwiches with them. She brought out a tin of Pop Biscuits, which were lovely. As soon as you bit them they went pop! and you suddenly found your mouth filled with new honey from the middle of the biscuits. Fanny took seven, one after another, for she was rather greedy. Bessie stopped her.

"*You'll* go pop if you eat any more!" she said.

"Do a lot of people live in this tree?" asked Jo.

"Yes, heaps," said Silky. "They move in and out, you know. But I'm always here, and so is the Angry Pixie, down below."

"Yes, we've seen *him*!" said Bessie. "Who else is there?"

"There's Mister Watzisname above me," said Silky. "Nobody knows his name, and he doesn't know it himself, so he's called Mister Watzisname. Don't wake him if he's asleep. He might chase you. Then there's Dame Washalot. She's always washing, and as she pours her water away down the tree you've got to look out for waterfalls!"

"This is a most interesting and exciting tree," said Bessie, finishing her cake. "Jo, I think we ought to go now, or we'll never get to the top. Good-bye, Silky. We'll come and see you again one day."

"Do," said Silky. "I'd like to be friends."

They all left the dear little round room in the tree and began to climb once more. Not long after they heard a peculiar noise. It sounded like an aeroplane throbbing and roaring.

"But there can't be an aeroplane in this tree!" said Jo. He peered all round—and then he saw what was making the noise. A funny old gnome sat in a deck-chair on a broad branch, his mouth wide open, his eyes fast shut—snoring hard!

"It's Mister Watzisname!" said Bessie. "What a noise he makes! Mind we don't waken him!"

"Shall I put a cherry in his mouth and see what happens?" asked Jo, who was always ready for a bit of mischief. The Faraway Tree was growing cherries all around for a change, and there were plenty to pick.

"No, Jo, no!" said Bessie. "You know what

Silky said—he might chase us. *I* don't want to fall out of the Faraway Tree and bump down from bough to bough, if *you* do!"

So they all crept past old Mister Watzisname, and went on climbing up and up. For a long time nothing happened except that the wind blew in the tree. The children did not pass any more houses or windows in the tree—and then they heard another noise—rather a peculiar one.

They listened. It sounded like a waterfall—and suddenly Jo guessed what it was.

"It's Dame Washalot throwing out her dirty water!" he yelled. "Look out, Bessie! Look out, Fanny!"

Down the trunk of the tree poured a lot of blue, soapy water. Jo dodged it. Fanny slipped under a broad branch. But poor old Bessie got well splashed from head to foot. How she shouted!

Joe and Fanny had to lend her their hankies. "I am most unlucky!" sighed Bessie. "That's twice I've been wetted to-day."

Up they went again, passing more little doors and windows, but seeing no one else—and at last they saw above them a vast white cloud.

"Look!" said Jo, in amazement. "This cloud has a hole in it—and the branches go up—and I believe we're at the very top of the tree! Shall we creep through the cloud-hole and see what land is above?"

"Let's!" cried Bessie and Fanny—so up they went.

V

THE ROUNDABOUT LAND

One big broad branch slanted upwards at the top of the Faraway Tree. Jo climbed on to it and looked down—but he could see nothing, for a white mist swirled around and about. Above him the enormous thick white cloud stretched, with a purple hole in it through which the topmost branch of the Faraway Tree disappeared.

The children felt tremendously excited. At last they were at the very top. Jo carefully pulled himself up the last branch. He disappeared into the purple hole. Bessie and Fanny followed him.

The branch came to an end and a little ladder ran through the cloud. Up the children went—and before they knew what had happened, there they were out in the sunshine, in a new and very strange land.

They stood on green grass. Above them was a blue sky. A tune was playing somewhere, going on and on and on.

"It's the sort of tune a roundabout plays, Jo," said Bessie. "Isn't it?"

It was—and then, suddenly, without any warning at all, the whole land began to swing round! The children almost fell over, so suddenly did the swing-round begin.

"What's happening?" said Bessie, frightened.

The children felt terribly giddy, for trees,

distant houses, hills, and bushes began to move round. They too felt themselves moving, for the grass was going round as well. They looked for the hole in the cloud—but it had disappeared.

"The whole land is going round and round like a roundabout!" cried Jo, shutting his eyes with giddiness. "We've passed over the hole in the clouds—we don't know where the top-most branch of the Faraway Tree is now—it's somewhere beneath this land, but goodness knows where!"

"Jo! But how can we get back home again?" cried Fanny, in a fright.

"We'll have to ask some one for help," said Jo. The three began to walk away from the patch

31

of green field in which they were standing. Bessie noticed that they had been standing on a ring of grass that seemed darker than the grass around. She wondered why it was. But she had no time to say anything, for really it was dreadfully difficult to walk properly in a land that was going round and round like a proper roundabout all the time!

The music went on and on too, hurdy-gurdy, hurdy-gurdy. Jo wondered where it came from, and where the machinery was that worked the strange Roundabout Land.

Soon they met a tall man singing loudly from a book. Jo stopped him, but he went on singing. It was annoying.

"Hie-diddle-ho-diddle, derry-derry down!" shouted the man, whilst Jo tried to make himself heard.

"How can we get away from this land?" Jo shouted.

"Don't interrupt me, hie-diddle, ho-diddle!" sang the man, and he beat time with his finger. Jo caught hold of the bony finger and shouted again.

"Which is the way out of this land, and what land is it?"

"Now you've made me lose my time," said the tall man crossly. "I shall have to begin my song again."

"What is this land, please?" asked Fanny.

"It's Roundabout Land," said the tall man. "I should have thought any one would have guessed that. You can't get away from it. It goes round and round always, and only stops once in a blue moon."

"There must have been a blue moon when *we* climbed into it!" groaned Jo. "It had certainly stopped then."

The man went off, singing loudly. "Hie-diddle, ho-diddle, derry-derry-down!"

"Silly old diddle-derry!" said Fanny. "Really, we do seem to meet the most peculiar people!"

"What I'm worried about is getting home," said Bessie. "Mother will be anxious if we are not back when she is. What shall we do, Jo?"

"Let's sit down under this tree and have a bit more to eat," said Jo. So they sat down, and munched solemnly, hearing the roundabout music going on all the time, and watching the distant hills and trees swinging round against the sky. It was all very strange.

Presently a pair of rabbits lolloped up and looked at the children. Fanny loved animals and she threw a bit of cake to them. To her surprise one of the rabbits picked up the cake in its paw and nibbled it like a monkey!

"Thanks!" said the rabbit. "It's a change from grass! Where do you come from? We haven't seen you before, and we thought we knew every one here. Nobody new ever comes to Roundabout Land."

"And nobody ever gets away," said the other rabbit, smiling at Fanny, and holding out its paw for a bit of cake too.

"Really?" said Bessie, in alarm. "Well, we are

new to it, for we only came about an hour ago. We came up the Faraway Tree."

"What!" cried both rabbits at once, flipping up their long ears in amazement. "Up the *Faraway* Tree, did you say? Goodness, you don't mean to say that's touching this land?"

"Yes, it is," said Bessie. "But I expect, as this land is swinging round and round, that the topmost branch might be almost anywhere underneath it — there's no way of finding out."

"Oh yes, there is!" said the first rabbit excitedly. "If we burrow down a little way, and make a hole, we can see whereabouts the Faraway Tree is underneath, and we can wait for it to come round again, when the Land swings above it."

"Well, we came up from the tree just where the grass was rather darker than the rest," said Bessie. "I noticed that. Do you suppose that as the Roundabout Land swings round, it will come back to the same place again, and we could slip down the topmost branch?"

"Of course!" said the rabbits. "We can easily burrow down that green patch of grass, and wait for the Land to turn round just over the tree again. Come on, quickly, there's no time to lose!"

All of them jumped up and sped off. Bessie knew the way and so did the rabbits. Soon they were back in the field where the ring of dark grass stood. There was no opening now, leading through a cloud down to the tree. It had gone.

The rabbits began to dig quickly. Soon they found the ladder that led upwards. Then they made such a big hole that the children could see down it to the large white cloud that swirled below the Roundabout Land.

"Nothing there yet," said the first rabbit, getting out a handkerchief and wiping his dirty front paws. "We must wait a bit. I only hope the Land hasn't swung on and passed the Faraway Tree altogether!"

The roundabout music went on and on, and then suddenly it began to slow down. One of the rabbits peeped out of the hole below and gave a shout.

"The Land has stopped going round—and the Faraway Tree is just near by—but we can't reach it!"

The children peered through the cloud below the ladder and saw quite clearly that the Faraway Tree was very near—but not near enough to jump on. Whatever were they to do?

"Now don't try to jump," warned the rabbits, "or you'll fall right through the cloud."

"But what shall we *do*?" asked Bessie, in despair. "We *must* get on the tree before we swing away again!"

"I've got a rope," said one of the rabbits suddenly, and he put his hand into a big pocket and pulled out a yellow rope. He made a loop in one end and then threw it carefully at the topmost branch of the nearby tree. It caught and held! Good!

"Fanny, slip down the rope first," said Jo. "I'll hold this end."

So Fanny, rather afraid, slid down the yellow rope to the tree—and then, just as she got there, the Roundabout music began to play very loudly and quickly, and the Roundabout Land began to move!

"Quick! Quick!" shouted Fanny, as the land swung nearer to the Faraway Tree. "Jump! Jump!"

They jumped—and the rabbits jumped after them. The Roundabout Land swung off. The big white cloud covered everything. The children and the rabbits clung to the topmost branch and looked at one another.

"We look like monkeys on a stick," said Jo, and they all began to giggle. "My goodness, what an adventure! I vote we don't come up here again."

But, as you may guess, they did!

VI

MOON-FACE AND THE SLIPPERY-SLIP

The children clung to the top branches of the Faraway Tree, whilst the rabbits slid down a bit lower. They could still hear the gay music of the Roundabout Land as it swung round overhead.

"We'd better get home," said Jo, in rather a quiet voice. "It's been just a bit too exciting."

"Come on then," said Bessie, beginning to

climb down. "It will be easier to get down than it was to climb up!"

But Fanny was very tired. She began to cry as she clung to her branch. She was the youngest, and not so strong as Jo and Bessie.

"I shall fall," she wept. "I know I shall fall."

Jo and Bessie looked at one another in alarm. This would never do. There was such a long way to fall!

"Fanny dear, you simply *must* try!" said Jo gently. "We've got to get home safely."

But Fanny clung to her branch and wept great tears. The two rabbits looked at her, most upset. One put his paw into her hand. "I'll help you," he said.

But Fanny wouldn't be helped. She was tired out and afraid of everything now. She wept so loudly that two birds nearly flew off in fright.

Just as the others were really in despair, a small door flew open in the trunk of the tree not far below, and a round moon-like face looked out.

"Hey there! What's the matter?" shouted the moon-faced person. "A fellow can't get any sleep at all with that awful noise going on!"

Fanny stopped crying and looked at Moon-Face in surprise. "I'm crying because I'm frightened of climbing down the tree," she said. "I'm sorry I woke you up."

Moon-Face beamed at her. "Have you got any toffee?" he asked.

"Toffee!" said every one in surprise. "What do you want toffee for?"

"To eat, of course," said Moon-Face. "I just thought if you had any toffee to give me I'd let you slide down my slippery-slip—you get down to the bottom very quickly that way, you know."

"A slide all the way down the Faraway Tree!" cried Jo, hardly believing his ears. "Good gracious! Who ever would have thought of that!"

"*I* thought of it!" said Moon-Face, beaming again just like a full moon. "I let people use it if they pay me toffee."

"Oh!" said the three children, and looked at one another in dismay, for none of them had any toffee. Then Jo shook his head.

"We've no toffee," he said. "But I've a bar of chocolate, a bit squashy, but quite nice."

"Won't do," said Moon-Face. "I don't like chocolate. What about the rabbits? Haven't they got any toffee either?"

The rabbits turned out their pockets. They had a very curious collection of things, but no toffee.

"Sorry," said Moon-Face, and slammed his door shut. Fanny began to cry again.

Jo climbed down to the door and banged on it. "Hie, old Moon-Face!" he shouted. "I'll bring you some lovely home-made toffee next time I'm up the tree if you'll let us use your slippery-slip."

The door flew open again, and Moon-Face beamed out. "Why didn't you say so before?" he asked. "Come in."

One by one the rabbits and the children climbed down to the door and went in. Moon-Face's house in the tree was very peculiar. It was one round room, and in the middle of it was the beginning of the slippery-slip that ran down the whole trunk of the tree, winding round and round like a spiral staircase.

Round the top of the slide was a curved bed, a curved table, and two curved chairs, made to fit the roundness of the tree-trunk. The children were astonished, and wished they had time to stay for a while. But Moon-Face pushed them towards the slide.

"You want a cushion each," he said. "Hie you, rabbit, take the top one and go first."

One of the rabbits took an orange cushion and set it at the top of the slide. He sat down on it, looking a little nervous. "Go on, hurry up!" said Moon-Face. "You don't want to stay all night, do you?" He gave the rabbit a hard push, and the rabbit slid down the slippery-slip at a tremendous pace, his whiskers and ears blown backwards. Jo thought it looked a lovely thing to do. He went next.

He took a blue cushion, sat on it at the top of the slide and pushed off. Down he went on his cushion, his hair streaming backwards. Round and round and round went the slippery-slip inside the enormous trunk of the old tree. It was quite dark and silent, and lasted a very long time, for the Faraway Tree was tremendously tall. Jo enjoyed every second.

When he came to the bottom his feet touched a sort of trap-door in the trunk at the foot, and the trap flew open. Jo shot out and landed on a big tuft of green moss which was grown there to make a soft landing-place. He sat there, out of breath— then he got up quickly, for he didn't want Bessie or Fanny landing on top of him.

Bessie went next. She flew down on a fat pink cushion, gasping for breath, for she went so fast. Then Fanny went on a green cushion, and then the other rabbit. One by one they shot out of the strange little trap-door, which closed itself tightly as soon as the slider had gone through.

They all sat on the ground, getting their breath and laughing, for it really was funny to shoot down inside a tree on a cushion.

The rabbits stood up first. "We'd better be going," they said. "So pleased to have met you!"

They disappeared down the nearest burrow, and the children waved good-bye. Then Jo stood up.

"Come on," he said, "we really must get home. Goodness knows what the time is!"

"Oh, what a lovely way of getting down the Far-away Tree that was!" said Bessie, jumping to her feet. "It was so quick!"

"I loved it," said Fanny. "I'd like to climb the tree every single day just so that I could slide down that glorious slippery-slip. I say—what do we do with the cushions?"

At that moment a red squirrel, dressed in an old jersey, came out of a hole in the trunk.

"Cushions, please!" he said. The children gathered them up and handed them to the squirrel one by one. They were getting quite used to hearing animals talk to them now.

"Are you going to carry all these cushions up the tree to Moon-Face?" asked Fanny, in wonder.

The squirrel laughed. "Of course not!" he said. "Moon-Face lets down a rope for them. Look— here it comes!"

A rope came slipping down between the branches. The squirrel caught the end of it and tied the bundle of cushions firmly on to the rope. He gave three tugs, and the rope swung upwards again, taking the cushions with it.

"Good idea!" said Jo, and then they all turned to go home, thinking, as they walked, of the strange and exciting things that had happened that day.

They came to the ditch and jumped across. They went down the lane and through their little back-gate. By the time they reached the cottage they were ready to drop with tiredness. Their mother and father were not yet home.

Bessie sleepily made some bread-and-milk. They undressed whilst the milk was heating, and then ate their supper sitting in their beds.

"I'm not going up the Faraway Tree again," said Fanny, lying down.

"Well, *I* am!" said Jo. "Don't forget we promised old Moon-Face some home-made toffee! We can climb up to his house, give him the toffee, and slide down that slippery-slip again. We don't need to go into any land at the top of the tree."

But Bessie and Fanny were fast asleep. And very soon Jo was too—dreaming of the strange Faraway Tree, and the curious folk who lived in its enormous trunk!

VII

BESSIE MAKES SOME TOFFEE FOR MOON-FACE

The children talked about nothing else but the Faraway Tree and its queer folk for days after their adventure. Bessie said they must certainly keep their promise to take toffee to Moon-Face.

"Promises must never be broken," she said. "I will make some toffee if mother will let me have some treacle. Then when it's done you can take it to Moon-Face, Jo."

Mother said they could make toffee on Wednesday, when the grocer came and brought their goods. So on Wednesday Bessie set to work making the best toffee she could.

She set it in a pan on the stove. It cooked beautifully. When it had cooled and was set nice and hard, Bessie broke it up into small pieces. She put them into a paper bag, gave one piece each to the others, and popped one into her own mouth.

"I'll have to go at night, I think," said Jo. "I shan't get any time off this week, I know. We're so busy with the garden now."

So that night, when the moon was shining brightly in the sky overhead, Jo slipped out of bed. Bessie and Fanny woke up and heard him. They hadn't meant to go with him, but when they saw the moonlight shining everywhere and thought of that exciting Faraway Tree, they felt that they simply *couldn't* stay behind! Wouldn't you have felt that too?

They dressed quickly and whispered through Jo's door. "We're coming too, Jo. Wait for us!"

Jo waited. Then they all three slipped down the creaky stairs and out into the moonlit garden. The shadows were very black indeed, just like ink. There was no colour anywhere, only just the pale, cold moonlight.

They were soon in the Enchanted Wood. But, dear me, it was quite, quite different now! It was simply alive with people and animals! In the very dark parts of the wood little lanterns were hung in rows. In the moonlit parts there were no lanterns, and a great deal of chattering was going on.

Nobody took any notice of the children at all. Nobody seemed surprised to see them. But the children were most astonished at everything!

"There's a market over there!" whispered Jo to Bessie. "Look! There are necklaces made of painted acorns and brooches made of wild roses!"

But Bessie was looking at something else—a dance going on in the moonlit dell, with fairies and pixies chattering and laughing together. Sometimes, when they were tired of dancing on their feet, partners would fly in the air and dance there in the moonlight.

Fanny was watching some elves growing toadstools. As fast as the toadstool grew, an elf laid a cloth on it and put glasses of lemonade and tiny biscuits there. It was all like a strange dream.

"Oh, I *am* glad we came!" said Bessie, in

delight. "Who would have thought that the Enchanted Wood would be like this at night?"

They wasted a great deal of time looking at everything, but at last they got to the Faraway Tree. And even here there was a great difference! The whole tree was hung with fairy lights and glittered softly from branch to branch, rather like a very enormous Christmas Tree.

Jo saw something else. It was a stout rope going from branch to branch, for people to hold on to when they wished to go up the tree.

"Look at that!" he said. "It will be much easier to go up to-night. All we'll have to do is just to hold on to the rope and pull ourselves up by it! Come on!"

Other folk, and some animals too, were going up the tree. Not to the land at the top, but to visit their friends who lived in the trunk of the enormous old tree. All the doors and windows were open now, and there was a great deal of laughing and talking going on.

The children climbed up and up. When they came to the window of the pixie who had been so angry with them last week because they had peeped in, they found that he was in a very good temper now, sitting smiling at his open window, talking to three owls. But Jo didn't think they had better stop, in case the pixie remembered them and threw water over them again.

So on they went holding on to the thick rope, climbing very easily. They came to Silky's house, and called her. She was baking over her stove.

"Hallo!" she said, looking up and smiling. "So here you are again—just in time, too, because I'm baking Pop Biscuits, and they are most delicious hot!"

Her silky golden hair stood out round her tiny face, which was red with baking. Jo took out his bag of toffees.

"We're really taking them to Moon-Face," he said, "but do have one!"

Silky took one and then gave them three hot Pop Biscuits each. My goodness, how lovely they were, especially when they went pop in the children's mouths!

"We mustn't stop, Silky dear," said Bessie. "We've still a long way to go up the tree."

"Well, look out for Mother Washalot's washing-water again, then," said Silky. "She's dreadful at night. She knows there are a lot of people up and down the tree, and she just loves to soak them with her dirty water!"

The children went on up. They passed Mister Watzisname, still fast asleep and snoring in his chair, and dodged quickly behind a branch when they heard Dame Washalot's water sloshing down. Nobody got even splashed this time! Fanny laughed.

"This really is the funniest tree I ever knew," she said. "You simply never know what's going to happen!"

They pulled themselves up and up by the rope and came at last to the top. They knocked on Moon-Face's yellow door. "Come in!" yelled a voice, and in they went.

Moon-Face was sitting on his curved bed, mending one of his cushions. "Hallo!" he said. "Did you bring me that toffee you owe me?"

"Yes," said Jo, handing him the bag. "There's a lot there, Moon-Face—half to pay you for last week's slippery-slide, and half to pay you if you'll let us go down again to-night."

"Oh my!" said Moon-Face, looking with great delight into the bag. "What lovely toffee!"

He crammed four large pieces into his mouth and sucked with joy.

"Is it nice?" said Bessie.

"Ooble-ooble-ooble-ooble!" answered Moon-Face, quite unable to speak properly, for his

46

teeth were all stuck together with the toffee! The children laughed.

"Is the Roundabout Land at the top of the Faraway Tree?" asked Jo.

Moon-Face shook his head. "Oooble!" he said.

"What land is there now?" asked Fanny.

Moon-Face made a face, and screwed up his nose. "Oooble-ooble-ooble-ooble-ooble!" he said very earnestly.

"Oh dear, we shan't be able to get anything out of him at all whilst he's eating toffee," said Bessie. "He'll just ooble away. What a pity! I *would* have liked to know what strange land was there to-night."

"I'll just go and peep!" said Jo, jumping up. Moon-Face looked alarmed. He shook his head, and caught hold of Jo. "Oooble-ooble-ooble!" he cried.

"It's all right, Moon-Face, I'm only going to peep," said Jo. "I shan't go into the land."

"OOBLE-OOBLE-OOBLE!" cried Moon-Face in a fright, trying his best to swallow all the toffee so that he could speak properly. "Ooble!"

Jo didn't listen. He went out of the door with the girls, and climbed up the last branch of the Faraway Tree. What strange land was above it this time? Jo peered up through the dark hole in the cloud, through which a beam of moonlight shone down.

He came to the little ladder that ran up the hole in the cloud. He climbed up it. His head poked out into the land at the top. He gave a shout.

"Bessie! Fanny! It's a land of ice and snow! There are big white bears everywhere! Oh, do come and look!"

But then a dreadful thing happened! Something lifted Jo right off the ladder—and he disappeared into the land of ice and snow above the cloud.

"Come back! Jo, come back!" yelled Moon-Face, swallowing all his toffee in his fright. "You mustn't even look, or the Snowman will get you!"

But Jo was gone. Bessie looked at Moon-Face in dismay. "What *shall* we do?" she said.

VIII

JO AND THE MAGIC SNOWMAN

Moon-Face was most upset to see Jo disappear. "I told him not to—I told him!" he groaned.

"You didn't," sobbed Fanny. "Your mouth was full of toffee and all you could say was 'Ooble-ooble-ooble!' And how could we know what that meant?"

"Where's Jo now?" asked Bessie, quite pale with shock.

Yes, indeed—where *was* Jo? Some one had lifted him right off the ladder, up into the Land of Ice and Snow! And there, strangely enough, the moon and the sun were in the sky at the same time, one at one side and the other opposite, both shining with a pale light.

Jo shivered, for it was very cold. He looked to

see what had lifted him off the ladder, and he saw in front of him a big strange creature—a snowman! He was just like the snowmen Jo had so often made in the wintertime—round and fat and white, with an old hat on his head and a pipe in his mouth.

"This is luck!" said the Snowman, in a soft, snowy sort of voice. "I've been standing by that hole for days, waiting for a seal to come up—and *you* came!"

"Oh," said Jo, remembering that seals came up to breathe through holes in the ice. "That wasn't a water-hole—that was the hole that led down the Faraway Tree. I want to go back, please."

"The hole has closed up," said the Snowman.

Jo looked—and to his great dismay he saw that a thick layer of ice had formed over the hole—so thick that he knew perfectly well he could never break through it.

"Whatever shall I do now?" he said.

"Just what I tell you," said the Snowman, with a grin. "This is splendid! In this dull and silent land there is nothing but polar bears, seals, and penguins. I have often wanted some one to talk to."

"How did you get here?" asked Jo, wrapping his coat firmly round him, for he was bitterly cold.

"Ah," said the Snowman, "that's a long story! I was made by some children long ago—and when they had finished me, they laughed at me and threw stones at me to break me up. So that night I crept away here—and made myself King. But what's the good of being King if you've only bears and things to talk to? What I want is a jolly good servant who can talk my language. And now *you've* come!"

"But I don't want to be your servant," said Jo indignantly.

"Nonsense!" said the Snowman, and he gave Jo a push that nearly sent him over. Then, on big, flat snow-feet he moved forward to where there was a low wall of snow.

"Make me a good house," he said.

"I don't know how to!" said Jo.

"Oh, just cut blocks of this stiff, icy snow and build them up one on top of another," said the Snowman. "When you've finished I'll give you a fur coat to wear. Then you won't shiver so much."

Jo didn't see that he could do anything but obey. So he picked up a spade that was lying by the wall and began to cut big bricks of the frozen snow. When he had cut about twenty he stopped and placed them one on the top of another till one side of the round house was made. Then he began to cut snow-bricks again, wondering all the time how in the world he would ever be able to escape from this strange land.

Jo had often built little snow-houses of soft snow in his garden at home during the winter. Now he made a big one, with proper snow-blocks, as hard as bricks. He quite enjoyed it, though he did wish the girls were there too. When he had finished it, and made a nice rounded roof, the Snowman came shuffling up.

"Very nice," he said, "very nice indeed. I can just get in, I think."

He squeezed his big snow-body inside, and threw out a fur coat for Jo, made of white polar-bear skin. Jo put it on very thankfully. Then he tried to squeeze in after the Snowman, for he wanted to be out of the cold, icy wind.

But he was so squashed between the Snowman and the walls of the snow-house that he couldn't breathe.

"Don't push so," said the Snowman disagreeably. "Move up."

"I can't!" gasped poor Jo. He felt quite certain that he would be pushed right out of the snow-hut through a hole in the wall!

Just then there came a curious grunt at the doorway. The Snowman called out at once.

"Is that you, Furry? Take this boy to your home under the ice. He's a nuisance here. He keeps squashing me!"

Jo looked up to see who Furry was — and he saw a great white bear looking in. The bear had a stupid but kind look on his face.

"Oooomph!" said the bear, and pulled Jo out into the open air. Jo knew it was no use to struggle. Nobody could get away from a bear as big as that! But the bear was certainly kindly.

"Oooooomph?" he said to Jo, with a loud grunting noise.

"I don't know what you mean," said Jo.

The bear said no more. He just took Jo along with him, half carrying the little boy, for Jo

51

found the way very slippery indeed.

They came to a hole that led under the ice and snow. The bear pushed Jo down it—and to Jo's enormous surprise he found there was a big room underneath, with five bears there, big and little! It was quite warm there too—Jo was astonished, for there was no fire, of course.

"Ooooomph," said all the bears politely.

"Ooooomph!" said Jo. That pleased the bears very much indeed. They came and shook paws with Jo very solemnly and ooomphed all over him.

Jo liked the look of the bears much more than he liked the look of the Snowman. He thought perhaps they might help him to escape from this silly land of ice and snow.

"Could you tell me the way back to the Faraway Tree?" he asked the bears politely and clearly. The bears looked at one another and then ooomphed at Jo. It was quite clear that they didn't understand a word he said.

"Never mind," said Jo, with a sigh, and made up his mind to put up with things till he could see a way to escape.

The Snowman was a great nuisance. No sooner did Jo settle himself down for a nap, leaning his head against the big warm body of a bear, than there came a call from the snow-house.

"Hie, boy! Come here and play dominoes with me!"

So Jo had to go and play dominoes, and as the Snowman wouldn't let him come into the hut because he said he was squashed, Jo had to sit at the doorway and play, and he nearly froze to bits.

Then another time, just as he was eating a nice bit of fried fish that one of the bears had kindly cooked in oil for him, the Snowman shouted to him to come and make him a window in his house. And Jo had to hurry off and cut a sheet of clear ice to fit into one side of the snow-house for a window! Really, that Snowman was a perfect nuisance!

"I wish to goodness I'd never peeped into this silly land," thought Jo a hundred times. "It's a good thing the bears are so nice to me. I only wish they could say something else besides 'Oooomph.' "

Jo wondered what Bessie and Fanny were doing. Were they very upset when he didn't come back? Would they go home and tell their father and mother what had happened?

Bessie and Fanny *were* upset! They were in a great fright too. It had been dreadful to see poor Jo disappear through the cloud like that.

Moon-Face looked very solemn too. He could speak quite well now that he had swallowed all his toffee.

"We must rescue him," he said, his face shining like the full moon.

"How?" asked the girls.

"I must think," said Moon-Face, and he shut his eyes. His head swelled up with his thinking. He opened his eyes and nodded his head.

"We'll go to Goldilocks and the Three Bears," he said. "Her bears know the bears in the Land of

Ice and Snow. She might be able to help Jo that way."

"But where does Goldilocks live?" asked Bessie, in wonder. "I thought she was just a fairy-tale."

"Good gracious, no!" said Moon-Face. "Come on — we'll have to catch the train."

"What train?" asked Fanny, in astonishment.

"Oh, wait and see!" said Moon-Face. "Hurry now — go down the slippery-slip and wait for me at the bottom!"

IX

THE HOUSE OF THE THREE BEARS

Bessie took a cushion, put it at the top of the slide, and pushed off. Down she went, whizzzzzzzzzz! She shot to the bottom, flew out of the trap-door and landed on the cushion of moss. She had hardly got up before Fanny flew out of the trap-door too.

"You know, that slippery-slip is the greatest fun!" said Bessie. "I'd like to do that all day long!"

"Yes, if only we didn't have to climb all the way up the tree first," said Fanny.

The trap-door flew open and out shot Moon-Face on a yellow cushion. He put the three cushions together, whistled to the red squirrel who looked after them, and threw them to him. Then he turned to the waiting girls.

"There's a train at midnight," he said. "We shall have to hurry."

The wood was still bright with moonlight. The three of them hurried between the trees. Suddenly Bessie heard the chuffing of a train, and she and Fanny stopped in surprise. They saw a small train winding in and out of the trees, looking for all the world like a clockwork train made big! The engine even had a key still in its side!

There was a small station near. Moon-Face caught hold of the girls' hands and ran to it. The train was standing quite still there.

The carriages had tin doors and windows which didn't open, just like those of a clockwork train. Bessie tried her hardest to open a door, but it was no use. The train whistled. It was anxious to be off.

"Don't you know how to get into this train?" asked Moon-Face, with a laugh. "You *are* sillies! You just slide the roof off!"

As he spoke he pushed at the roof—and it slid off like the roof of a clockwork-train's carriage.

"I believe this is just a clockwork train made big," said Fanny, climbing over the side of the carriage and getting in at the roof. "I never saw such a funny train in my life!"

They all got in. Moon-Face couldn't seem to slide the roof on again properly, so he stood up inside the carriage, and when the train went off, Bessie and Fanny, who couldn't possibly see out of the tin windows, stood up and looked out of the roof instead. They did look funny!

At the next station, which was called "Rabbit Station," three rabbits got into their carriage and stared at them very hard. One was so like Bessie's own rabbit at home that she couldn't help staring back.

The second station was called "Crosspatch Station," and standing on the platform were three of the crossest-looking old women that the girls had ever seen. One of them got into their carriage, and the three golliwogs at once got out, and climbed into the next one.

"Move up!" said the Crosspatch angrily to Moon-Face. He moved up.

The Crosspatch was an uncomfortable person to travel with. She grumbled all the time, and her basket, which was full of prickly rose-sprays, kept bumping into poor Fanny.

"Here we are, here we are!" sang out Moon-Face, when they got to the next station, and the three of them got out gladly, leaving the Crosspatch grumbling away all to herself.

The station was called "Bears Station," and there were a great many teddy-bears about, some brown, some pink, some blue, and some white. When they wanted to talk to one another they kept pressing themselves in the middle, where their growl was, and then they could talk quite well. Fanny wanted to giggle when she saw them doing this. It did look so funny.

"Please, could you tell me the way to the Three Bears' House?" Moon-Face asked a blue teddy-bear politely.

The bear pressed himself in the middle and answered in a nice growly voice, "Up the lane and down the lane and around the lane."

"Thank you," said Moon-Face.

"It sounds a bit funny to me," said Bessie doubtfully.

"Not at all," said Moon-Face, leading them up a little honeysuckle lane. "Here we are, going *up* a lane—and now you see it goes downhill—so we're going down—and presently we'll turn a corner and go *around* the lane!"

He was right. They went up and then down and then around—and there in front of them, tucked into a woody corner, was the dearest, prettiest little house the girls had ever seen! It was covered with pink roses from top to bottom, and its tiny windows winked in the moonlight as if they had eyes.

Moon-Face knocked at the door. A sleepy voice cried "Come in!" Moon-Face opened the door and they all went in. There was a table in front of them, and on it were three steaming bowls of porridge, and round it were three chairs, one big, one middle-size, and one tiny.

"It's the House of the Three Bears all right!" whispered Bessie excitedly. It was just like seeing a fairy story come true!

"We're here!" said the voice from another room. Moon-Face went in with Bessie and Fanny. The other room was a small bedroom, with a big bed in it, a middle-sized bed, and a tiny cot. In the big bed lay a large brown bear, in the middle-sized one was a fat mother bear, and in the cot was a most adorable baby bear with the bluest eyes the girls had ever seen.

"Where's Goldilocks?" asked Moon-Face.

"Gone shopping," said the father bear.

"Where does she sleep when she's here?" asked Bessie, looking round. "And does she always live with you now?"

"Always," said the father bear, putting his big nightcap straight. "She looks after us very well. There's a market on to-night in the Enchanted Wood and she's gone to see if she can buy some porridge cheap. As for where she sleeps, well, she just chooses any of our beds, you know, and we cuddle up together then. But she likes the baby bear's bed best, because it's so soft and warm."

"She did in the story," said Fanny.

"What story?" asked the mother bear.

"Well—the story of the three bears," said Fanny.

"Never heard of it," said the three bears, all together, which really seemed rather extraordinary to Bessie and Fanny. They didn't like to ask any more questions after that.

"Here's Goldilocks now!" said the mother bear. The sound of a little high voice could be heard coming nearer and nearer. The baby bear sprang out of his cot and ran to the door in delight.

A pretty little girl with long, curling golden hair picked him up and hugged him. "Hullo, darling!" she said. "Have you been a good bear?"

Then she saw Bessie, Fanny, and Moon-Face, and stared at them in surprise. "Who are you?" she said.

Moon-Face explained about Jo, and how he had gone to the Land of Ice and Snow, where the big white bears lived.

"I'm afraid the Magic Snowman will make him a prisoner there," said Moon-Face. "And he'll have to live with the white bears. Could you get your three bears to come with us and ask the white bears to let Jo go free, Goldilocks?"

"But I don't know the way," said Goldilocks.

"*We* do!" said the father bear suddenly. "The white bears are cousins of ours. Moon-Face, if you can help us with a bit of magic, we can visit the Land of Ice and Snow in a few minutes!"

"Good gracious!" said Bessie, most astonished.

"But it's ever so far away, right at the top of the Faraway Tree!"

"That doesn't matter," said the father bear. He took down a large jar from the mantelpiece and filled it with water. He put into it a yellow powder and stirred it with a magpie's black-and-white feather.

Moon-Face put his hands into the water and began to sing a string of such strange words that Bessie and Fanny felt quite trembly. The water bubbled. It rose to the top of the jar. It overflowed and ran on to the floor. It turned to ice beneath their feet! A cold wind filled the little house and every one shivered.

Then Bessie looked out of the window—and what she saw there filled her with such amazement that she couldn't say a word, but just pointed.

Fanny looked too—and whatever do you think? Outside lay nothing but ice and snow—they were in the same land as Jo! Though how this had happened neither Bessie nor Fanny could make out.

"We're there," said Moon-Face, taking his hands out of the jar and drying them on his red handkerchief. "Can you lend us any coats, bears? We shall be cold here."

The mother bear handed them thick coats out of a cupboard. They put them on. The bears already had thick fur and did not need anything extra.

"Now to go and find Jo!" said Moon-Face. "Come on, bears—you've got to help!"

X

THE BATTLE OF THE BEARS

Goldilocks, the Three Bears, the girls, and Moon-Face all went out of the little cottage. How strange it seemed to see roses blossoming over the walls, when ice and snow lay all around!

"The thing is—*where* do we go to find the polar bears?" said Goldilocks.

"Over there, towards the sun," said the father bear. Bessie and Fanny were surprised to see both the moon and the sun shining in the sky. They followed the father bear, slipping and sliding, and holding on to one another. It was very cold, and their noses and toes felt as if they were freezing.

Suddenly they saw the little snow-house that Jo had built for the Magic Snowman.

"Look!" said the father bear. "We'd better make for that."

But before they got there a big white figure squeezed itself out of the snow-house and saw them. It was the Magic Snowman! As soon as he saw the Three Bears and the others, he began to shout loudly in a windy, snowy voice:

"Enemies! Enemies! Hie, bears, come and send off the enemies!"

"We're not enemies!" yelled Moon-Face, and Goldilocks ran forward to show the Snowman that she was a little girl. But Moon-Face pulled her back. He didn't trust that old Snowman!

The Snowman bent his big fat body down and picked up great handfuls of snow. He threw one at Goldilocks. She ducked down, and it passed over her and hit the baby bear.

"Ooooch!" he said, and sat down in a hurry. Then everything happened at once. A crowd of white polar bears hurried out of their underground home to the help of the Snowman, and soon the air was full of flying snowballs. The snow was hard, and the balls hurt when they hit any one. It wasn't a bit of good the girls shouting that they were friends, not enemies. Nobody heard them, and soon there was a fierce battle going on!

"Oh dear!" gasped Bessie, trying her best to throw straight. "This is dreadful! We shall never rescue Jo by behaving like this!"

But there really didn't seem anything else to be done! After all, if people are fighting you, you can't do much but defend yourself, and the Three Bears, and the girls, and Moon-Face felt very angry at having hard snowballs thrown at them.

Smack! Thud! Biff! Squish! The snowballs burst as they hit, and soon there was a great noise of angry "Ooomphs" from the white bears, and "Ooooches" from the teddy-bears, and yells from the children, and screeches from Moon-Face, who acted as if he were mad, hopping about and yelling and kicking up the snow as well as throwing it! His big fat face was a fine target for snowballs, and he was hit more than anybody else. Poor Moon-Face!

Now whilst this fierce battle was going on,

where do you suppose Jo was? As soon as he had heard the cry of "Enemies! Enemies!" he had hidden in a corner, for he didn't want to be mixed up in any fight. When he saw the white bears going out, and he was left all alone, he began at once to think of escaping.

He crept to the hole that led above-ground. The battle was some way off, so Jo did not see that the enemies were really his own friends! If he had he would have gone to join them at once.

"What a terrible noise they are all making!" he thought. "It sounds like a battle between gorillas and bears to me! I'm not going near them — I'd be eaten up or something! I shall just run hard the opposite way and hope I'll meet some one to help me."

So Jo, dressed in his bearskin, and looking just like a little white bear himself, crept off over the ice and snow, not seen by any one. He ran as soon as he thought he was out of sight. He ran and he ran and he ran.

But he met nobody. Not a soul was to be seen. Only a lonely seal lay on a shelf of ice, but even he dived below as soon as he saw Jo.

And then Jo stopped in the greatest astonishment and stared as if his eyes would fall out of his head. He had come to the cottage of the Three Bears, standing all alone in the middle of the ice and snow — and, of course, its roses were still blooming round it, scenting all the air.

"I'm dreaming!" said Jo. "I simply *must* be dreaming! A cottage — with roses — here in the middle of the snow! Well—I shall go and see who lives there. Perhaps they would give me something to eat and let me rest, for I'm very hungry and tired."

He knocked at the door. There was no answer. He opened the door and went in. How he stared! There was no one to be seen at all, but on the table stood three bowls of steaming porridge, one big, one middle-sized, and one small. It was rather dark, so Jo lighted a big candle on the table.

Then he sank down into the biggest chair—but it was far too big and he got up again. He sat down in the next sized chair—but that was too piled up with cushions, and he got up to sit in the smallest chair. That was just right, and Jo settled down comfortably—but alas, his weight was too much for it, and the chair broke to bits beneath him!

He looked at the delicious porridge. He tasted the porridge in the biggest bowl—it was much too hot and burnt his tongue. He tasted the next bowl —but that was far too sweet. But when he tasted the porridge in the little bowl, it was just right.

So Jo ate it all up! Then he felt so sleepy that he thought he really must rest. So he went into the bedroom and lay down on the biggest bed. But it was far too big, so he tried the middle-sized one. That was too soft and went down in the middle, so Jo lay down on the cot. And that was so small and warm and comfortable that he fell fast asleep!

All this time the battle was going on. The

Snowman was so big and the polar bears were so fierce that very soon the teddy-bears, the children, and Moon-Face were driven backwards.

Then a snowstorm blew up, and the snow fell so thickly that it was quite impossible to see anything. Moon-Face called out in alarm:

"Bears! Goldilocks! Bessie! Fanny! Take hold of each other's hands at once and don't let go. One of us might easily be lost in this storm!"

Every one at once took hands. The snow blew into their faces and they could see nothing. Bending forwards they began to walk carefully away from the white bears, who had stopped fighting now and were trying to find out where their enemies were.

"Don't shout or anything," said Moon-Face. "We don't want the white bears to hear us, in case they take us prisoners. They might not listen to the teddy-bears. Move off, and we'll look for some sort of shelter till this storm is over."

They were all very miserable. They were cold, rather frightened, and quite lost. They stumbled over the snow, keeping hold of one another's hands firmly. They went on and on, and suddenly Goldilocks shook off Moon-Face's hand and pointed in front of them.

"A light!" she said in astonishment. Every one stopped.

"I say! I SAY! It's our cottage!" shrieked the baby bear, in surprise and delight. "But who's inside? *Some* one must have lighted the candle!"

They all stared at the lighted window. Who

was inside the cottage? Could the Magic Snowman have found it? Or the polar bears? Was it an enemy inside — or a friend?

"Wheeeeeeeeew!" blew the wind, and the snow-flakes fell thickly on every one as they stood there, wondering.

"Ooooh!" shivered Moon-Face. "We shall get dreadful colds standing out here in the snow. Let's go in, and find out who's there."

So the father bear opened the door, and one by one they all trooped in, looking round the empty room, half afraid.

XI

MORE AND MORE SURPRISES

"There doesn't *seem* to be any one here!" said Bessie, cautiously looking round.

"Well, WHO lighted that candle?" asked Moon-Face, his big round face looking anxious. "*We* didn't leave it lighted!"

Suddenly the father bear gave an angry growl, and pointed to his chair. "Who's been sitting in *my* chair?" he said.

"And who's been sitting in *my* chair?" said the mother bear, pointing to hers.

"And who's been sitting in *my* chair and broken it all to bits?" squeaked the baby bear, in tears.

Bessie giggled. "This sounds like the story of

the Three Bears coming true!" she said to Fanny. "They'll talk about porridge next."

They did.

"Who's been eating *my* porridge?" said the father bear angrily.

"And who's been eating *my* porridge?" said the mother bear.

"And who's been eating mine, and gobbled it all UP?" wept the baby bear, scraping his spoon round the empty plate.

"It's all very mysterious," said Moon-Face. "*Some*body lighted the candle—*some*body sat in the chairs—*some*body ate the porridge. But who?"

"Not me this time," said Goldilocks. "I was

with you all the time we were snowballing, wasn't I, Bears?"

"You certainly were," growled the father bear, patting the little girl on the back. He was very fond of her.

"I wish we had found poor Jo," said Bessie. "Whatever will he be doing in this horrid cold land?"

"Do you suppose we ought to go out and look for him again?" said Fanny, shivering as she thought of the ice cold wind outside.

"No," said Moon-Face decidedly. "No one is going out of this cottage again till we're safely in the wood at home. I'm afraid we can't possibly rescue Jo now."

"What's that noise?" said Goldilocks suddenly. Everybody listened. *Some* one was snoring softly in the next room!

"We never thought of looking there," said Moon-Face. "Who can it be?"

"Sh!" said Goldilocks. "If we can catch him asleep, we can tie him up and make him a prisoner easily. But if he wakes up he might be fierce."

They tiptoed to the door of the bedroom. One by one they squeezed through.

"Who's been lying on *my* bed?" said the father bear, in a growly voice.

"Sh!" said Moon-Face crossly.

"Who's been lying on *my* bed?" said the mother bear.

"SH!" said every one.

"And who's been lying on *my* bed and is fast asleep there still?" said the baby bear.

Every one stared at the cot. Yes—there was some one there—some one in a white bearskin. Was it a polar bear?

"It's a white bear!" said Moon-Face, half frightened.

"Tie him up before he wakes," said the father bear. "He's an enemy now."

Goldilocks got a rope out of the kitchen cupboard. Moon-Face went one side of the cot, and the father bear went the other, the rope held between them. They nodded to one another. In a trice both bent down, caught hold of the sleeper, and twisted the rope tightly round him!

"He's caught!" cried Moon-Face joyfully.

Jo awoke with a jump. Who had got him? Had the Magic Snowman caught him again? He began to shout and struggle. Moon-Face tied him more tightly.

And then Bessie and Fanny saw his face, and yelled out loudly:

"Moon-Face! It's Jo! It's Jo! Oh, it's Jo!"

They rushed to the cot and flung their arms round Jo. The boy was too astonished to speak. He got out of the rope and hugged his sisters.

"How did you get here?" he asked.

"How did *you* get here?" cried Bessie and Fanny.

"Come into the kitchen and we'll all have some hot porridge and milk," said Goldilocks. "We can talk then and get warm."

So Jo went with the others, all chattering loudly

about everything. Goldilocks ladled out porridge into blue bowls, and made some cocoa. Soon every one was putting sugar or treacle on porridge and drinking cocoa. Jo poured some milk over his porridge and smiled joyfully at everybody.

"What an adventure this has been!" he said. "Shall I tell my tale first, or will you tell yours?"

He told his—and then Bessie told how Moon-Face had gone to the Three Bears for their help, and all about the fierce battle.

"It's a pity about the battle," said the father bear mournfully. "The white bears are cousins of ours, and have always been friendly—now they seem to be enemies."

"Let's hope they don't discover our cottage," said Goldilocks, eating her hot porridge. "Moon-Face, hadn't we better make some magic and get back to the wood?"

"Plenty of time, plenty of time," said Moon-Face, pouring himself out another cup of cocoa.

But, you know, there *wasn't* plenty of time. For just at that moment Goldilocks gave a scream and pointed to the window.

"Some one looked in!" she said.

"Don't be silly!" said Moon-Face.

"I'm not," said Goldilocks. "I tell you, *some-*body looked in! Who could it be?"

"The handle of the door is moving!" yelled Moon-Face, and he leapt to the door. In a trice he had locked it and bolted it.

The father bear got up and went to the window. He looked out into the snowstorm.

"I can't see anything," he said; and then he growled loudly, "Yes, I can—I can see the white bears! They have surrounded our cottage! *Now* what shall we do?"

"Well, they can't get in at the door, and they certainly *shan't* get in at the window," said Moon-Face, looking fierce. The door shook, but it held well. Some one battered on it.

"We shan't let you in!" yelled Jo.

"If any one tries to open the window or break it, I'll hit him with this kettle!" shouted Moon-Face, who had caught up the kettle and was dancing about with it.

"Moon-Face, that kettle has got hot water in it," said Fanny. "Do be careful. You dropped some on me."

"I'll pour it down the neck of any bear that dares to come in here!" yelled Moon-Face, spattering the room with steaming drops.

"Oh dear!" said Bessie. "Hide behind the bed, Fanny. It seems to me that Moon-Face is almost as dangerous as the bears."

The father bear dragged the big table across the door. Things were getting exciting. Jo and the girls were frightened, but they couldn't help feeling terribly thrilled too. Whatever was going to happen next?

"Oooomph! Oooomph!" boomed the big bears outside, but they couldn't get in at the door or window.

But they found another way! The chimney was wide and big, for the fireplace was one of the old-

71

fashioned kind and needed a wide chimney. One of the bears climbed up on to the roof, followed by three more. The first one slipped into the big chimney. Down he went, whoooosh! Down went another — and the third — and the fourth.

They landed with a crash on to the big hearth, and hurriedly jumped away from the flames of the fire.

"Surrender!" they cried to the startled children and bears. "Surrender! The Magic Snowman is outside! Let him in!"

XII

WHAT HAPPENED TO THE SNOWMAN

Every one stared at the big white bears in horror. No one had thought of the chimney. What a pity they hadn't stopped it up!

"I am going to let the Magic Snowman in," said the first white bear.

Then the father bear spoke up, in a very sorrowful voice.

"Cousin, why are we enemies? We have always been good friends up till now."

The four white bears looked at him and at the mother bear and baby bear in sudden amazement. They rushed at them with loud ooooomphy noises.

Jo thought they were going to fight the Three Bears, and he took up a jug from the table to help his friends. But no, the white bears were not going to fight—they were hugging the Three Bears as tightly as they could, and to the children's amazement tears were pouring down their furry faces!

"We didn't know it was you!" said the white bears. "Why, cousins, we would never have fought you if only we had known you were the Three Bears we love so much!"

"There, there!" said the mother bear, wiping the tears of a white bear off her fur. "It's all right. But for goodness' sake tell the other bears we're friends. We don't want the front door battered down."

Moon-Face opened the door and yelled out of it, "Bears! It's all right! This is the cottage of your cousins, the Three Bears! We're friends!"

But the white bears didn't answer or come in—instead a big white shape came up and squeezed through the door—the Magic Snowman!

A chill fell over the little room. The white bears were frightened of him, for he was their master. He shut the door and glared at every one out of his stone eyes.

"So even my own bears have gone over to the enemy!" he said. "Oho! What will you say if I turn you into ice and snow, every one?"

Nobody said anything. But, to Bessie's surprise, Moon-Face shut the door, and then went to the fire. He piled on three great logs and winked at Bessie.

The Snowman took up a white bear by the scruff of the neck and shook him.

"So you found your voices, did you?" he said. "Didn't I tell you that you were only to say 'Oooomph' and not speak a word to any one? I won't have bears that talk!"

He picked up another white bear and shook him. "So you are friends with my enemies, are you?" he said.

The room became very hot. Jo took off his coat. So did the others. Moon-Face slyly put on another log. The fire crackled and shot great flames up the chimney. Fanny wished she could take off everything, she was so hot.

"Whatever does Moon-Face think he is doing, making the room so hot?" she thought crossly. But just as she was about to tell him to put the guard round the fire, he winked at her, and she said nothing. Moon-Face had some queer plan that he was carrying out.

The Snowman went on and on, grumbling and threatening. Every one listened and said nothing. Moon-Face poked the fire and it blazed up higher.

"Now this is what I'm going to do," said the Magic Snowman. "I'm going to take this nice little cottage for my own—and I shall live here. All of you others can live in a snow-house and freeze, for all I care. You will all wait on me and do whatever I say."

"Yes," said everybody. They all knew now what Moon-Face's plan was. He meant to make the room so hot that the Magic Snowman would melt. Clever old Moon-Face! A little trickle of water began to run from the Snowman's broad white

74

back, which was near the fire. Moon-Face pointed to it secretly and grinned.

Fanny thought Moon-Face's beaming face looked so funny that she began to giggle. She really couldn't help it. Goldilocks giggled too, and stuffed her handkerchief into her small mouth. The baby bear gave a high squeak of a giggle and then wept bitterly because the Snowman cuffed him.

"How dare you laugh!" shouted the Snowman angrily. "Outside, all of you! Outside! This is my cottage now, and not one of you shall stay here."

They all crowded outside except Moon-Face, who crouched behind a big chair, determined not to leave the fire in case it burnt low.

Outside it was bitterly cold. The white bears quickly dug up the snow and made a high wall to shelter the others from the wind. They crouched there, cuddling close to one another for warmth. The big white bears wrapped their furry arms round the children and warmed them beautifully. Jo thought they were very kind indeed.

They waited and they waited. They could see smoke pouring from the chimney of the cottage and they knew that Moon-Face must be keeping up the fire. The bears ooomphed every now and again, and the children whispered to one another.

Then suddenly the door of the cottage was flung open and Moon-Face stood there, his big face beaming like a full moon.

"You can come back now!" he shouted. "It's quite safe!"

They all crowded back to the cottage. Jo looked for the Snowman—but he was gone! There was nothing to show that he had been there, except a very large puddle of water.

"He melted very quickly," said Moon-Face. "He may have been very magic and very powerful—but he was just made of snow after all. So he melted like a real snowman on a sunny morning."

The polar bears ooomphed with delight. They had hated being servants to the Snowman.

"We'll say good-bye to you now," they said to the Three Bears. "This cottage is cosy but it's too hot for us. Come and see us again whenever you like. Good-bye!"

Every one hugged them good-bye, and Jo felt quite sad to see them go. Moon-Face shut the door after them.

"Now we'll get back home," he said. "I'm a bit tired of this land. Come on, Bears, help me to get the cottage back safely!"

He didn't do the same magic as before. He drew a circle on the floor in blue chalk and the Three Bears stood inside, holding paws. Moon-Face danced round them, singing strings of queer magic words. A wind rose up, and the cottage rocked. Darkness came down, and for a moment no one could see anything at all.

Then gradually the darkness went and the wind blew no more. The sun shone warmly in at the window. Bessie gave a shout.

"I say! We're back in the little woody corner where we first saw the cottage! And it's daytime now, not nighttime!"

"Well, we've been having this adventure all night long!" said Moon-Face, with a laugh. "It's sunrise now—the night has gone. You'd better hurry off home, children, or you'll be scolded for leaving your beds at night."

They hugged Goldilocks, and shook hands with the Three Bears. "We'll come back and see you sometime," said Fanny. "Thank you so much for all your help!"

Goldilocks and the bears stood at the door and waved good-bye as Moon-Face hurried the three children away down the lane to catch the train back to the Enchanted Wood. It wasn't long before they had got to the station, waited for a train, slid off the roof and settled down in a carriage.

When they got to the Enchanted Wood they said good-bye to Moon-Face, and Fanny gave him a kiss for being such a help. He was so pleased that he went red all over his enormous face, and Bessie laughed.

"You look like the setting sun now," she said. "You really ought to be called Sun-Face!"

"Good-bye, and see you soon, I hope!" called Moon-Face. Off went the children home, and got into bed just about an hour before their mother called them to get up. My goodness, they *were* sleepy all that day!

XIII

MOON-FACE GETS INTO TROUBLE

The children didn't really feel that they wanted to go to any of the lands at the top of the Faraway Tree for a little while. It was a bit too exciting to climb through the clouds and see what was above them!

But they did want to see their friends in the Tree, especially dear old Moon-Face.

So the very next time they had a day to themselves they set off through the Enchanted Wood to the Faraway Tree. There was no rope to guide them this time. It was only at night that the rope was swung through the boughs to help the wood-folk up and down.

The children began to climb up. Every door and window in the tree seemed shut to-day, and not a soul was about. It was quite dull climbing up the tree. Even when they reached Silky's house, that was shut too, and they couldn't hear Silky singing or anything. They knocked, but there was no answer.

So on they went up to Moon-Face's, keeping a good look-out for Mother Washalot's dirty water to come swishing down on them. But not even her water appeared that day! It all seemed very quiet and peaceful.

They reached Moon-Face's house at the top of the tree and rapped at his door. Nobody opened.

But inside they could quite well hear somebody crying. It was very mysterious.

"It doesn't sound like Moon-Face," said Fanny, puzzled. "Let's go in and see who it is."

So they opened the door and went in. And it was Silky, sitting in a corner crying bitterly!

"Whatever's the matter?" cried Jo.

"And where's old Moon-Face?" asked Fanny.

"Oh dear!" sobbed Silky. "Moon-Face has been thrown up into some dreadfully queer land at the top of the Faraway Tree because he was rude to Mister Watzisname down below."

"What! That old man who's always sitting in a chair and snoring?" said Bessie, remembering that they hadn't seen him that day. "Whatever did Moon-Face do?"

79

"Oh, he was very naughty," wept Silky. "So was I. You see, we heard Mister Watzisname snoring as usual, and we crept up to him and saw that his mouth was wide open. And, oh dear, we popped a handful of acorns into it, and when he woke up he spluttered and popped, and then he caught sight of us hiding behind a branch."

"Goodness! Did you really dare to do such a naughty thing!" cried Bessie. "No wonder he was angry!"

"Moon-Face is dreadfully bad sometimes," said Silky, wiping her eyes. "He makes me naughty too. Well, we ran away up the tree to Moon-Face's house. I got in safely—but Moon-Face didn't. And Mister Watzisname caught hold of him and threw him right through the hole in the clouds into the land that is there to-day."

"Good gracious! Well, can't he get back?" said Fanny, in alarm. "He can climb down the ladder, surely, back into the tree?"

"Yes, he could," said Silky, "but, you see, Mister Watzisname is sitting on the ladder ready to catch him, spank him, and throw him back. So what's the use of that?"

"What land is up there to-day?" asked Jo.

"The Land of the Old Saucepan Man," said Silky. "He lives there in his cottage with his pots and pans, and is quite harmless. But, you see, Mister Watzisname will sit on the ladder till the land swings round and another one comes. Then Moon-Face won't be able to get back, and he may be lost for ever!"

"Oh dear!" said Jo in dismay, and the girls stared at Silky in despair, for they were very fond of old Moon-Face now.

"Isn't there anything we can do?" asked Jo at last.

"Well, there's just one hope," said Silky, fluffing out her lovely golden hair. "The Old Saucepan Man is a great friend of Mister Watzisname's. If he knew his land was at the top of the Faraway Tree to-day he might come along and have a cup of tea with Mister Watzisname, and then Moon-Face could slip down the ladder back here!"

"Oh," said the children, and looked at one another. They could quite well see that this meant one or all of them going up that ladder again and getting into another queer land.

"I'll go," said Bessie. "After all, Moon-Face helped us last time. We must help him now."

"We'll all three go," said Jo. So they set off up the topmost branch to the little ladder. There they found Mister Watzisname sitting reading his newspaper and smoking an enormous pipe that sent clouds of smoke out of the hole in the clouds.

"Please can we pass?" asked Bessie timidly.

"No, you can't," said Mister Watzisname rudely.

"Well, we've got to," said Jo. "So if we tread on your feet you must excuse us."

Mister Watzisname simply wouldn't move. He really was a very cross old man. He slapped each of the children as they squeezed past him, and they were very glad when they had climbed through the hole and were in the land above.

"So this is the Land of the Saucepan Man," said Fanny, when they were standing on the grass safely. "What a funny little land!"

It was. It was an island floating in what seemed a sea of white. It really wasn't much bigger than a large field. Bessie went to the edge and looked over.

"Gracious!" she said, in alarm. "It's like a cliff —and the sea is a big white cloud. Don't go too near the edge, anybody. It wouldn't be nice to fall off!"

"Hie! Hie!" suddenly yelled an excited voice. They turned round—and saw Moon-Face waving to them, and running hard towards them. "Hie! How did you get here?"

"Hallo! We came to see what we could do for you," said Jo. "We heard what had happened. Old Mister Watzisname is sitting on the ladder still, waiting for you. But Silky says this is the Land of the Saucepan Man, who is a great friend of Mister Watzisname's—so we've come to see him and ask him if he'll go and have tea with his friend. Then you can slip down safely and go home."

"Oooh, good!" said Moon-Face joyfully. "I didn't know what land this was, and goodness me, I was quite afraid of falling off it, it's so small. Where do you suppose the Old Saucepan Man lives?"

"I can't imagine!" said Jo, looking round. All he could see was a very large stretch of grass, with no house and nobody at all in sight. Where in the world could the Saucepan Man live?

"We'll have to go carefully all round this funny little land," said Bessie. "His house must be somewhere. But we'd better hurry, for you never know when the land will swing away from the Faraway Tree—and we don't want to live in this queer little place for ever!"

They began to walk round the land. Presently they came to a cliff that was not quite so steep as the others. They peered over it. Jo pointed to some things stuck in the cliff.

"Whatever are those?" he said.

"They look like some sort of steps down the cliffside," said Bessie.

"They're *saucepans*!" said Fanny suddenly. "Yes—*saucepans*—with their handles stuck firmly into the cliff, and the pan part to tread on. How queer!"

"Well, this must be the way down to the Saucepan Man's house," said Jo, excited. "Come on. Be careful, girls, or you may fall and roll right over the edge of this land."

So, very carefully, they began to climb down the cliff, treading on the saucepans stuck into the earth. It really was rather funny!

They got down at last. And then they heard a very curious noise indeed! It was a sound of crashings and bangings and clatterings and clangings! The children were quite alarmed.

"The noise is coming from just round the corner," said Jo.

They crept very cautiously to the corner and peeped round.

There they saw a crooked little house with a saucepan for a chimney. The noise came from inside the house. The children crept to the window and looked in.

And inside they saw the strangest little man they had ever seen, dancing the strangest dance! He had saucepans and kettles hung all over him, he wore a saucepan for a hat, and he crashed two saucepans together as he danced!

"Do you think he is dangerous?" said Jo, in a whisper.

XIV

THE FUNNY OLD SAUCEPAN MAN

"I don't think he's at all dangerous," said Fanny. "He has quite a kind face."

"Let's tap at the window," said Bessie. So she tapped. But the Saucepan Man took no notice. He just went on dancing away, crashing his saucepans together.

Jo tapped loudly. The Saucepan Man caught sight of him at the window and looked most astonished. He stopped dancing and went to the door.

"Come in and dance," said he.

"Oh no, thank you," said Jo. "We've just come to ask you out to tea."

"Ask me for a bee?" said the Saucepan Man,

looking surprised. "I'm so sorry, but I don't keep bees, only saucepans."

"Not bees," said Jo. "To ask you out to TEA."

"But I don't want to go to sea," said the Saucepan Man. "I don't like the water at all. Never did. Very kind of you, I'm sure, but I hate the sea."

"Not the sea, but TEA, TEA, TEA!" cried Jo.

"Oh, tea," said the Saucepan Man. "Well, why didn't you say that before? Then I should have understood."

"I *did* say it before," said poor Jo.

"What? Shut the door?" said the Saucepan Man. "Certainly, if you want to. Give it a push."

"He can't hear very well," said Fanny. "He must be deaf."

"No, I'm not," said the Saucepan Man, hearing perfectly all of a sudden. "Not a bit deaf. Only sometimes when my saucepans have been crashing round me rather a lot I get noises in my ears afterwards. But I'm not deaf."

"I'm glad of that," said Jo politely.

"Cat? No, I haven't got a cat," said the Saucepan Man, looking all round. "Did you see one?"

"I didn't say anything about a cat," said Jo patiently.

"You did. I heard you," said the Saucepan Man, vexed. "I don't encourage cats. I keep mice instead. I shall look for that cat."

And then, with his saucepans clanging round him he began to look for a cat that certainly wasn't

85

there. "Puss, Puss, Puss!" he called. "Puss, Puss, Puss!"

"There's no cat in your house!" shouted Moon-Face.

"Mouse? Where did you see a mouse?" said the old man, alarmed. "I wouldn't like one of my mice to be caught by your cat."

"I tell you we haven't GOT a cat!" cried Jo, feeling quite cross. "We've come to tell you about your friend, Mister Watzisname."

For a wonder the Saucepan Man heard Jo, and he at once stopped looking for the cat. "Mister Watzisname!" he cried. "Where is he? He's a great friend of mine."

"Well, wouldn't you like to go and have tea with him then?" said Jo.

"Yes, certainly I would," said the Saucepan Man. "Please tell me where he is."

"He's sitting on the ladder leading from the Faraway Tree to your land," shouted Jo. "He's waiting there."

"Yes—for me!" said Moon-Face, in a whisper.

"Sh!" said Fanny. The Saucepan Man gave a yell of joy when he heard where his old friend was, and he set off for the cliff, shouting in delight.

"Hurrah! I've come to the Faraway Tree! And I can see my friends again! And Mister Watzisname is waiting for me to have tea with him! Come on! Come on!"

Up the cliff he went, treading on the saucepan steps, his own saucepans and kettles rattling and

86

banging all round him. The children and Moon-Face followed. The Saucepan Man ran helter-skelter to the hole that led down to the topmost branch of the Faraway Tree, dropping a few saucepans on the way.

When he got there he peered down and saw Mister Watzisname sitting on the ladder, watching for Moon-Face. But the Saucepan Man didn't know that, of course! He thought that his friend was waiting for *him*!

"Hie, hie, hie!" he yelled, dropping a saucepan on top of Mister Watzisname in his excitement. "Hie, old friend!"

Mister Watzisname watched the saucepan bouncing off his foot, down the branch of the Faraway Tree, and wondered who it would hit. He looked up in amazement when he heard his friend's shouts.

"Saucepan!" he yelled. "Dear old Saucepan! Fancy seeing *you*!"

"Glue?" said the Saucepan Man, suddenly hearing all wrong again. "Glue?—No—I've not got glue with me. But I can soon make some for you."

"Still the same silly old Saucepan, aren't you!" cried Mister Watzisname. "Come down here. I didn't say anything about glue. Come and have a cup of tea with me. The kettle's boiling."

"I don't want oiling," said the Saucepan Man, though he really sounded as if he did, he was so full of clangs and clatters! "I'll come and have tea and a talk with you. Hurrah!"

He put his foot on the ladder, but unfortunately he stepped on a kettle that had got round his leg, and down he went, clatter, bang, crash, smash, clang! Mister Watzisname caught at him as he went past, and down he went too, rolling off the ladder, down the branch, past Moon-Face's door and down the tree!

"There they go!" said Moon-Face, in delight. "All mixed up with kettles and saucepans. What a joke! They'll give old Mother Washalot a fright if they fall into her wash-tub!"

The children laughed till they cried. The Old Saucepan Man was really so funny, and they couldn't *imagine* what people in the tree would think as he rolled down with such a clanging and banging.

"It's quite safe to go down now," said Jo, peering down the ladder. "They've disappeared. I shouldn't wonder if they're at the bottom of the tree by now. Come on, Moon-Face."

So down the ladder they all went, slid down the topmost branch, and opened Moon-Face's door. Silky was still there, looking scared out of her life. She gave a scream of joy when she saw them.

"Why are you looking so frightened?" asked Moon-Face, giving her a hug.

"Oh, goodness, a thunderbolt or something fell out of the sky just now and rolled crashing down the tree!" said Silky.

"That was only the Saucepan Man and Mister Watzisname," said Jo, laughing, and he told her the whole story. Silky laughed till her sides ached.

She ran out of the door and peeped down the tree.

"Look!" she said, pointing. "Can you see far down there, between the branches?"

They all looked—and they saw Mister Watzisname and the Old Saucepan Man climbing painfully up to Mister Watzisname's home, both talking together at the top of their voices.

"They've forgotten all about us," said Jo joyfully. "Now for goodness' sake, Moon-Face, don't go putting acorns into Watzisname's mouth again. Let's have something to eat, and then we must go home down your slippery-slip."

So they all five sat round Moon-Face's funny room and ate some Pop biscuits that Silky fetched, and drank acornade, which was made of acorns and was most delicious. Then it was time for the children to go, and they chose cushions, sat at the top of the big tree-slide, pushed off and flew down the inside of the tree, sliding round and round and round till they shot out of the trapdoor at the bottom on to the cushion of moss. Then they ran home as fast as they could, for they were late.

"I expect the Old Saucepan Man's gone back to his queer little land by now," said Jo, as they turned in at their gate.

But he hadn't. He came to see them the very next day, his saucepans clanging so loudly that Mother looked quite alarmed.

"Whoever in the world is that?" she said, as the Saucepan Man came in at the gate.

XV

THE SAUCEPAN MAN GOES TO THE WRONG LAND!

Mother and the children stared at the queer Old Saucepan Man as he came in at the gate. He wore an extra-large-sized saucepan for a hat, and, as he came, he knocked two pans together, and sang a queer nonsense song that went like this:

> "Two beans for a pudding,
> Two cherries for a pie,
> Two legs for a table,
> With a hi-tiddle-hi!"

At the last "hi" he banged on the door with a saucepan. Mother opened it.

"Don't make such a noise," she said.

"No, I haven't seen any boys," said the Saucepan Man, and he clashed his pans together so loudly that Mother jumped. Then he caught sight of the children and waved to them eagerly. "Oh, there you are! Moon-Face told me where you lived."

"Whoever is he?" said Mother, in wonder. "Children, is this queer old man all right?"

"Oh yes," said Jo, hoping that Mother wouldn't ask them too many questions. "Can we take him into the garden and talk to him, Mother? He makes such a noise indoors."

"Very well," said Mother, who wanted to get on with her washing. "Take him along."

"A song?" said the Saucepan Man obligingly. "Did you say you wanted a song, Madam?" he began to sing again, and crashed his pans in time to his song:

> "Two pigs for the pantry,
> Two shoes for the horse,
> Two hats for the tigers,
> Pink ones, of course."

The children hustled him out into the back-garden. "That's a very, very silly song of yours," said Bessie loudly, right in his ear. "What's it called?"

"It hasn't got a name," said the Saucepan Man. "I make it up as I go along. It's quite easy. Every line but the last one begins with the word 'two'. I'm sorry you think it's silly." He looked rather offended. Then suddenly he smiled again and said, "I've come to ask you all to tea in my cottage."

"Will Mister Watzisname be there?" asked Jo, who wasn't at all anxious to meet him again.

"Yes, you'd better brush your hair," said the Saucepan Man, looking at Jo's untidy hair.

"I said 'Will Mister Watzisname be there?'" said Jo loudly.

"Something in the air?" said the Saucepan Man, and he looked up anxiously. "Not a thunder-storm, you don't mean?"

"No, I certainly don't mean a thunderstorm,"

said Jo, with a groan. "Yes—we'll come. We must ask Mother first."

Mother said they could go, though she still didn't very much like the look of the Old Saucepan Man.

"Good-day," she said to him, as he went off with the children.

He really was a most peculiar sight, but he had such a twinkly sort of face that the three children couldn't help liking him and trusting him.

They soon came to the Faraway Tree, and saw that Moon-Face had thought of a marvellous idea. He had borrowed Mother Washalot's biggest washing-basket and let it down on a rope. Then, as soon as they were all safely in it, he and Silky meant to haul them up, to save them the long, long climb!

"That's a really good idea!" said Jo, delighted. They all climbed in. It was a bit difficult to get the Saucepan Man in too, but they managed at last, though he seemed to find it most uncomfortable to sit on his saucepans.

"Up we go!" shouted Jo as the basket swung upwards through the branches. It ran very smoothly, and the children enjoyed the strange ride. At last they came to a big branch and stepped out on it. It was quite near Moon-Face's house at the top. Moon-Face was there, winding up the rope, a grin on his big, shining face.

"How did you like *that*?" he asked. The Saucepan Man looked at him anxiously.

"Cat?" he said. "Another cat? Dear me! I hope

it won't escape into my land. I've got my mice there."

"Now he'll go looking for cats again," said Bessie. And sure enough the Saucepan Man began to peer here and there, calling, "Puss, Puss, Puss!"

"Never mind him," said Moon-Face. "Go on up the ladder. He wants you to go to tea with him in his funny saucepanny house!"

"Come on, Saucepan Man!" called Jo. "If you want us to come to tea, we'd better go!"

The Saucepan Man heard. He stopped looking for cats and ran up the ladder. With a bound he was through the hole in the cloud, and right above.

And no sooner had he gone out of sight than he began to yell:

"Oooooh! Oooohoww! Wowooo!"

The children listened in alarm. "Whatever's the matter with him?" said Jo.

Crash! Bang! Clang! Smash!

"He sounds as if he's rolling about on all his kettles and saucepans!" said Bessie. "What can he be doing?"

"Ooooohooow!" shouted the Saucepan Man above them. "Stop it! Ow! Stop it!"

"Somebody must be attacking him!" cried Jo. He leapt up the ladder. "Come on, every one! We'll soon send any enemies off!"

He shot up the ladder, followed by Bessie, Fanny, and Moon-Face. They all clambered through the hole in the clouds and stood in the land above.

But oh, my goodness me! It was no longer the Land of the Saucepan Man, that tiny, little, cloud-edged country! It was another land altogether!

"My land's gone!" shrieked the Saucepan Man. "I didn't know it had! This is somewhere else! Oooooh!"

No wonder he said "Oooooh!" The bit of flat field he was standing on suddenly gave a shiver like a jelly, and then just as suddenly tipped itself up so that it made a hill! The Saucepan Man rolled down it at top speed, all his pans clattering like milk-churns on a railway station!

"This is Rocking Land," said Moon-Face, in

dismay. "Quick! Come back to the ladder and get down the hole before we have forgotten where it is! Hie, Saucepan Man, come over here to us!"

"Bus, did you say?" shouted back the Saucepan Man, picking himself up and looking round. "I can't see a bus. I'd like to catch one."

"Come here to US, to US, to US!" shouted Jo, in despair. "The hole through the clouds is here. We must get back again quickly!"

The Saucepan Man began to run downhill to them, but the ground all round suddenly tipped backwards, and he and the children and Moon-Face found themselves running downhill away from the hole in the clouds where the precious ladder was! They tried to stop. They tried to walk back up the sudden hill—but the land tipped up all the more and at last they couldn't stand up, but had to lie down.

Then they began to roll downhill. How they rolled! Over and over and over, with the Saucepan Man making a frightful clatter with all his pans.

"Ooooooh! Ow! Ooooooh!" cried every one.

"We've lost the hole!" shouted Jo. But before he could say any more he bumped into a bush that knocked all the breath out of him! Soon every one lay in a heap at the bottom of the hill, and tried to get back their breath.

"Now we're in a fix," said Bessie, dusting herself. "What a very tiresome land to have got into. Does it do this sort of thing all the time, Moon-Face?"

"Oh, yes," said Moon-Face. "It never stops. It

heaves up here and sinks down there, and rocks to and fro and gives sudden little jerks. People do say there's a giant just underneath, trying to throw the land off his back."

XVI

WHAT HAPPENED IN THE ROCKING LAND

The Rocking Land was really most annoying. No sooner did the children stand up very carefully and try to walk a few steps, than the earth beneath them either fell away or tipped up or slanted sideways in a very alarming manner!

Then down they all went, rolling over and over! The Saucepan Man made a tremendous noise and almost cried when he saw how battered his saucepans and kettles were getting.

"Moon-Face!" yelled Jo. "How can we get out of here? Don't you know?"

"We can only get out by going down the ladder that leads to the Faraway Tree!" shouted back Moon-Face, who was busy rolling down a little hill that had suddenly appeared. "Look for it all the time, or we'll never get away from here. As soon as the Rocking Land leaves the place where the Faraway Tree is, we've no way of escape!"

That gave the others a shock. The thought of living in a land of bumps and jerks and jolts was not at all pleasant! They all began to look about for the hole through which they had come into the Rocking Land.

Soon the earth began to do something rather different. It heaved up and down very quickly as if it were breathing fast! When it heaved up it threw the children and the others into the air. When it breathed downwards they rolled into holes and stayed there. It was all dreadfully uncomfortable.

"I'm getting awfully bruised!" shouted Bessie. "For goodness' sake let's find a place on this land where it's not quite so fidgety. I think we must be on the worst bit."

As soon as the earth stopped heaving about they all ran hard to where a wood grew. And there, just inside the wood, they saw a shop!

It was such a surprising thing to see in the Rocking Land that they all stopped and stared.

"What does it sell?" said Jo.

"You don't feel *well*?" said the Saucepan Man, quite deaf for a time. "I don't either. I feel as if I've been on a ship in a very rough sea!"

"I said 'What does the shop *sell*?'" said Jo.

"No, I didn't hear a bell," said the Saucepan Man, looking round as if he expected to see an enormous bell somewhere.

Jo gave it up. He looked hard at the shop. It was just a wide stall, with a tiny house behind it. No one seemed to be there, but smoke rose from the chimney, so some one must live there, Jo thought.

"Come on," he said to the others. "Take hold of hands so that we keep together. We'll go and see this funny shop and see if we can get help."

They walked up to it. The stall was piled high with cushions of all colours, each one with a rope tied to it.

"How funny!" said Bessie, in astonishment. "Cushions with ropes! Now who in the world would want to buy cushions here?"

"Well, *I* would, for one!" said Moon-Face at once. "My goodness, if I had a fine fat cushion tied on the front of me, and another tied at the back, I wouldn't mind being bumped about nearly so much!"

"Oh, of course—that's what the cushions and ropes are for," said Bessie joyfully. "Let's buy some—then we shan't get bruised any more."

Just then a sharp-nosed little woman, with cushions tied all round her, came out of the tiny house and looked at the children. She even had a small cushion tied on her head, and she did look funny.

Fanny giggled. She was a dreadful giggler. The woman looked cross and glared at Fanny.

"Do you want to buy my cushions?" she asked.

"Yes, please," said Moon-Face, and he took out his purse. "How much are they?"

"Five silver pieces of money each," said the woman, her little green eyes shining as she saw Moon-Face's purse. Moon-Face looked at her in dismay.

"That's much too high a price!" he said. "I've

98

only got one silver piece. Have you got any money, Saucepan Man?"

"No, I don't sell honey," said the Saucepan Man.

"MONEY, MONEY, MONEY!" shouted Moon-Face, showing the Saucepan Man his purse.

"Oh, money," he said, taking out an enormous purse from one of his kettles. "Yes, I've plenty."

But the great big purse was empty! The Saucepan Man stared at it in dismay.

"All my money must have fallen out when I rolled about," he said. "There's nothing left!"

The children had no money at all. The sharp-nosed little woman shook her head when Moon-Face begged her to lend them cushions in return for his silver piece.

"I don't lend anything," she said, and went back to her house, banging the door loudly.

"It's too bad," said Moon-Face, taking hold of Jo's hand and walking off gloomily. "Mean old thing! Oh, look—there are some more people— all wearing cushions!"

Sure enough they met plenty of queer-looking folk, well-padded with cushions of all colours, sizes, and shapes, walking carefully about the paths. One man wore a big eiderdown all round him, which Bessie thought was a fine idea.

"The Rocking Land is quite peaceful for a change," she said to Fanny. But she spoke too soon—for even as she said these words the earth began to heave up, first one way and then another!

Over went the children and everybody else and rolled here and there and up and down as the land poked up first in one place and then in another.

"Oooooh!" groaned the children.

"Wish I had a few cushions!" cried Moon-Face, who had rolled on his big nose and bent it sideways.

Crash! Clank! Bang! went the Saucepan Man, rolling on his kettles and pans very noisily.

"Oooh, look!" suddenly shrieked Bessie, in delight, and pointed back towards the little wood where the shop was. The earth there had risen steeply upwards, and all the cushions were rolling down towards the children!

"Grab them!" shouted Jo. So they all caught the cushions, and began to tie them firmly round them. My goodness, it did make a difference when they rolled about!

"It serves that mean old woman right!" said the Saucepan Man as he tried his hardest to put cushions round himself and his saucepans.

Suddenly one of the people of the Rocking Land gave a frightened shout and clutched hold of a nearby tree. A strange wind blew with a low, musical sound.

"Now what's going to happen?" cried Moon-Face.

"Get hold of a tree! Get hold of a tree!" shouted the people round about. "When the wind makes that sound it means that the whole of the land is going to tip up sideways and try to roll every one

100

off. Your only hope is to catch hold of a tree!"

Sure enough the land was slowly tipping up — not in bits and pieces as it had done before, but the whole of it! It was very extraordinary. Moon-Face was frightened. He tried to get to a tree, and he shouted to the others.

"Catch hold of a tree! Hurry up!"

But not one of them could, for they had left the wood behind them and were in a field. Slowly and surely the land tipped sideways, and the children and Moon-Face and the Old Saucepan Man began to roll downhill on their cushions. They were not bruised but they were very much frightened. What would happen to them if they rolled right off the land?

Down they went and down, nearer and nearer to the edge of the Rocking Land — and then, quite suddenly, Moon-Face disappeared! One moment he was there — the next he was gone! It was most peculiar.

But in half a minute they heard his voice, lifted up in the greatest excitement. "I say, I say, every one! I've fallen down the hole to the ladder that leads to the Faraway Tree, quite by accident. I'll throw my cushions up through the hole so you'll know where it is. Roll to it if you can! Make haste!"

Then the children and the Saucepan Man saw two cushions appear, and they knew where the hole was. They did their best to roll to it, and one by one they got nearer and nearer.

Bessie rolled right down it, plop, and caught

hold of the ladder as she fell. Jo rolled down next, missed the ladder and landed with a bump on the top branch of the Faraway Tree.

The Saucepan Man rolled to it next, but he got stuck in the hole, for he was now so fat with cushions as well as kettles and saucepans that he could hardly get through.

"Oh, quick, quick, quick!" shouted Jo. "Get in, Saucepan Man, get in! Poor Fanny will roll right past the hole if you don't make haste!"

The Saucepan Man saw Fanny rolling past. Poor Fanny! Once she rolled past the hole she couldn't possibly roll back again, for it would be all uphill. Quick as lightning the Saucepan Man reached out his hand and caught hold of one of the ropes that tied Fanny's cushion to her back. She stopped with a jerk.

One of the Saucepan Man's kettles gave way and he fell through the hole to the ladder, making a tremendous noise. Moon-Face caught him — and then the Saucepan Man gave a tug at Fanny's rope and she came down the hole too, landing softly on the top branch of the Faraway Tree, for she was well-padded with her cushions!

"Well, thank goodness you found the hole, Moon-Face!" said every one, still looking rather scared. "*What* an adventure!"

XVII

AN INVITATION
FROM MOON-FACE AND SILKY

Nobody had really enjoyed their visit to the Rocking Land, which had been a mistake, anyhow. They sat in Moon-Face's house, untying their cushions from their backs and fronts, and looking at all the bruises they had got.

"What shall we do with these cushions?" said Bessie.

"Moon-Face could do with them, I expect," said Fanny. "He uses such a lot for his slippery-slip, don't you, Moon-Face?"

"Yes, they'd do very well," said Moon-Face, his big face beaming joyfully. "Some of mine are getting very old and worn. We can't possibly give them back to that cross old woman in the Rocking Land, so we might as well put them to some use here."

"Right," said Jo, and he handed Moon-Face his two cushions. Every one else did the same. Moon-Face was pleased. He poured lemonade for every one, then handed round a tin of sweets.

"I don't feel as if I ever want to see what land is at the top of the Faraway Tree again," said Jo, as he munched a peculiar toffee sweet which seemed to get bigger in his mouth instead of smaller.

"Neither do I," said Bessie.

103

"I certainly never will!" said Fanny. "It seems as if there are never any lands there worth visiting. They are all most uncomfortable."

"Except *my* little land," said the Saucepan Man, rather mournfully. "I was always very comfortable there."

Jo's sweet was now so big that he couldn't say a word. Then it suddenly exploded in his mouth, went to nothing, and left him feeling most astonished.

"Oh dear—did you take a Toffee Shock?" said Moon-Face, noticing Jo's surprised face. "I'm so sorry. Take another sweet."

"No, thank you," said Jo, feeling that one Toffee Shock was quite enough. "I think we'd really better be going. It must be getting late."

"What's going to happen to the Old Saucepan Man now that he's lost his land?" asked Bessie, picking up a yellow cushion, ready to slide down the tree.

"Oh, he'll live with Mister Watzisname," said Moon-Face. "Hallo—he's taken a Toffee Shock by mistake. Watch him, do!"

They all watched. The Saucepan Man's Toffee Shock had got enormous, and was about to explode. It did—and went to nothing in his mouth. The Saucepan Man blinked his eyes and looked so astonished that every one shouted with laughter.

"That was a Toffee Shock you were eating!" said Moon-Face.

"A Coffee Clock?" said the Saucepan Man, even more surprised. "Dear me!"

"Come on!" said Bessie, giggling. "It's time we went. See you another day, Moon-Face! Good-bye, Saucepan Man!"

She shot off down the slide, round and round and out of the trap-door at the bottom. Then Fanny slid off, and then Jo.

"Good-bye," he called. "Good-bye!"

Mother was astonished to see their bruises. "Whatever have you been doing?" she said. "I shan't let you go to tea with the Saucepan Man again if you come home like this. And how dirty your clothes are!"

Jo longed to tell Mother about the Rocking Land and their adventure there, but he felt sure she would think he was making it all up. So he said nothing and went off to change his dirty clothes.

Things did not go very well the next week. Father lost some money one night, and Mother could not get very much washing to do. So that money was very scarce, and the children did not have as much to eat as they would have liked.

"If only we could have a few hens!" sighed Mother. "They would at least give us eggs to eat. And a little goat would give us milk."

"And what I want is a new garden spade," said Father. "Mine broke yesterday and I can't get on with the garden. It is very important that we should grow as many vegetables as possible, for we can't afford to buy them!"

To make things worse their father was very cross with them for having spoilt their clothes the day they had gone off with the Saucepan Man.

"If that's the way you treat the only nice clothes you have, you will just stay at home and not go out at all!" he scolded.

The children did not like being scolded, and Bessie mended their clothes as nicely as she could. Two weeks went by, and the children had not even had two hours to themselves to go and see Moon-Face.

"He'll be wondering what has happened to us," said Fanny.

Moon-Face certainly *was* wondering. He had waited each day and each night to see the children, and he and Silky wondered what was the matter.

"We'll send the Barn Owl with a note to tell the children to come quickly," said Silky at last. So she slipped down the Faraway Tree to the hole where the Barn Owl lived. She knocked at his door, and he pecked it open.

"What is it?" he asked, in a hoarse voice.

"Oh, Barny dear, will you take this note to the children at that little cottage over by the wood?" asked Silky, in her sweetest voice. "You're going out hunting to-night, aren't you?"

"Yes," said the Barn Owl, and he took the note in one of his great clawed feet. "I'll take it."

He slammed his door shut behind him and rose into the air on great creamy wings, as silent as the wind. He flew to the children's cottage. They were in bed, asleep.

Barny sat on the tree outside and screeched loudly. The children awoke with a jump.

"Whatever's that?" said Bessie.

106

Jo came into their room. "Did you hear that?" he asked. "Whatever could it be?"

The Barn Owl screeched again. He certainly had a dreadful voice. The children jumped. Jo went bravely to the window and looked out. "Is anyone being hurt?" he called.

"Meeeeeeeeeeeee!" screeched the owl again, and Jo nearly fell out of the window with fright! The Barn Owl spread his great soft wings and flew to Jo. He dropped the note on to the window-sill, screeched again, and flew off into the night to look for mice and rats.

"It was a Barn Owl!" said Jo. "It left a note! Quick, light your candle and let's see what the letter says!"

107

They lighted the candle and crowded round the note. This is what it said:

"DEAR, JO, BESSIE, AND FANNY,

"Why don't you come to see us? Are you cross? Please come soon, because there is a wonderful land at the top of the tree now. It is the Land of Take-What-You-Want. If you want anything, you can usually get it there for nothing. Do come, and we'll all go together. Love from

MOON-FACE AND SILKY."

"Oooooh!" said Fanny, excited. "The Land of Take-What-You-Want! Well, *I'd* like to get a few hens."

"And *I'd* like a goat!" said Bessie.

"And *I'd* like a new spade for Father!" said Jo. But then he frowned. "I'd quite made up my mind not to go up to any more of those strange lands," he said. "You simply never know what might happen there. We'd better not go."

"Oh, *Jo*!" cried Bessie. "Do let's! After all, if there *is* a nice land we might as well visit it."

"Sh! You'll wake Mother!" said Jo. "We'll see to-morrow what happens. If we can get some time to ourselves we'll go and ask Moon-Face if the land is really *safe* to go to. Now we'd better go to bed and sleep."

But they didn't sleep much! No—they were all wondering what the Land of Take-What-You-Want was like, and if they were really going to visit it to-morrow!

XVIII

THE LAND OF TAKE-WHAT-YOU-WANT

The next day was very fine. The children helped their mother to clean the whole house down, and Jo proudly brought in some fine peas and lettuces from the garden, which he had grown himself. Mother was pleased.

"You can go off after lunch by yourselves if you like," she said. "You have been very good to-day."

The children looked at one another in glee. Just what they hoped! Good!

"Come on!" said Jo, after lunch. "We won't waste any time!"

"What about tea?" said Bessie. "Oughtn't we to take some with us?"

"I should think we can get tea all right from the Land of Take-What-You-Want!" said Jo, with a grin.

So they all ran off, waving good-bye to Mother. They were soon in the Enchanted Wood, hearing the trees whispering secretly to one another, "Wisha-wisha-wisha!"

They ran through the bushes and trees to the Faraway Tree, and up they went. When they passed the window of the Angry Pixie, Jo peeped in, just for fun. But he was sorry he did, for the Angry Pixie was there, and he threw a basin of soup all over poor Jo!

"Oh!" said Jo in dismay, as he saw his shirt all

splashed with soup. "You wicked pixie!"

The Angry Pixie went off into peals of delighted laughter, and banged his window shut.

"Pooh! You do smell of onions now, Jo!" said Bessie, wrinkling up her nose. "I hope the smell soon goes off."

Jo wiped himself down with his handkerchief. He said to himself that one day he would pay the Angry Pixie out!

"Come on," said Fanny impatiently. "We'll never get there!"

They passed the Barn Owl's door and saw him sitting inside, fast asleep. They came to Silky's little yellow door too, but she wasn't in. There was a note pinned on her door which said, "OUT. BACK SOON."

"She must be with Moon-Face," said Jo. "Now just look out for Dame Washalot's water, every one."

It was a good thing he reminded them, for not long after that a fine waterfall of soapy suds came pouring down. Fanny screamed and dodged, so did Bessie. Jo got some on his shirt and he was cross.

"Never mind!" said Fanny, with a giggle. "It will wash off some of the onion soup, Jo!"

They went on up, and came to Mister Watzisname's. He was, as usual, sitting in a deck-chair, fast asleep, with his mouth open. And beside him, also fast asleep, was the Old Saucepan Man, looking most uncomfortable, draped round as usual with saucepans and kettles.

"Don't wake them," whispered Jo. "We'd better not stop and talk." So they crept by them—but just as they had got to the next branch the Saucepan Man woke up.

He sniffed hard, and poked Mister Watzisname. "What's the matter, what's the matter?" said his friend.

"Can you smell onions?" asked the Saucepan Man. "I distinctly smell them. Do you suppose the Faraway Tree is growing onions anywhere near us to-day? I love onion soup."

Jo and the girls laughed till they cried. "It's the onion soup on your shirt that the Saucepan Man smelt," said Bessie. "My goodness! They'll spend all the afternoon looking for onions growing on the Faraway Tree!"

They left the two funny old men and went climbing up—and they got nicely caught by Dame Washalot's second lot of water. She was doing a great deal of washing that day, and she emptied a big wash-tub down just as the three children were nearly underneath.

"Slishy-sloshy-slishy-sloshy!" The water came pouring down and soaked all the children. They gasped and shook themselves like dogs. "Quick!" said Jo. "We will go as fast as we can to Moon-Face's house and borrow some towels from him. This is dreadful!"

They arrived at Moon-Face's at last. Old Moon-Face and Silky rushed out to hug them—but when they saw how dripping wet the children were, they stopped in surprise.

111

"Is it raining?" said Moon-Face.

"Have you had a bath in your clothes?" asked Silky.

"No. It's just Dame Washalot's water as usual," said Jo crossly. "We dodged the first lot, but we got well caught by the second lot. Can you lend us towels?"

Moon-Face grinned and pulled some towels out of his curved cupboard. As the children rubbed themselves down, Moon-Face told them all about the Land of Take-What-You-Want.

"It's a marvellous land," he said. "You are allowed to wander all over it and take whatever you want for yourselves without paying a penny. Every one goes there if they can. Do come and visit it with me and Silky."

"Is it quite, quite safe?" asked Jo, rubbing his hair dry.

"Oh yes," said Silky. "The only thing is we must be careful not to stay there too long, in case it leaves the Faraway Tree and we can't get down. But Moon-Face says he will sit by the ladder and give a loud whistle if he sees any sign of the Land moving away."

"Good," said Jo. "Well, there are plenty of things we want. So let's go now, shall we?"

They all climbed up the topmost branch to the great white cloud. The ladder led through the hole as usual to the land above. One by one they climbed it and stood in the strange country above the magic cloud.

It was indeed strange! It was simply crowded

with things and people! It was quite difficult to move about. Animals of all kinds wandered here and there; sacks of all sorts of things, from gold to potatoes, stood about; stalls of the most wonderful vegetables and fruit were everywhere; and even such things as chairs and tables were to be found waiting for any one to take them!

"Good gracious!" said Jo. "Can we really take anything we want?"

"Anything!" said Moon-Face, settling himself down by the ladder in the cloud. "Look at those gnomes over there! They mean to take all the gold they can find!"

The children looked where Moon-Face was pointing. Sure enough there were four gnomes, hauling at all the sacks of gold in sight. One by one they staggered off to the ladder with them and disappeared down to the Faraway Tree. Other fairy folk hunted for the different things they wanted—dresses, coats, shoes, singing birds, pictures, all kinds of things! As soon as they had found what they were looking for, they rushed off to the ladder in glee and slipped down it. Moon-Face found it fun to watch them.

The others wandered off, looking at everything in surprise.

"Do you want a nice fat lion, Jo?" asked Silky, as a large lion wandered by and licked Silky's hand.

"No, thank you," said Jo, at once.

"Well, what about a giraffe?" said Silky. "I believe they make fine pets."

"You believe wrong then," said Bessie, as a tall giraffe galloped past like a rocking-horse. "Nobody in their senses would want to keep a giraffe for a pet."

"Oh, look!" cried Fanny, as she came to a shop in which stood a great many large and beautiful clocks. "Do let's take a clock back home!"

"No, thank you," said Jo. "We know what we want, and we'll take that and nothing else."

"I think *I* should like a clock," said Silky, and she picked up a small clock with a very nice smily face. It had two feet underneath, which waggled hard as Silky picked up the clock.

"It wants to walk!" said Bessie, with a scream of laughter. "Oh, do let it, Silky. I've never seen a clock walk before!"

Silky put the clock down and it trotted beside them on its big flat feet. The children thought it was the funniest thing they had ever seen. Silky was very pleased with her new clock.

"Just what I've always wanted," she said. "I shall keep it at the back of my room."

"You don't suppose it will stay there, do you, Silky?" asked Bessie. "It will wander round and about and poke its nose into everything you're doing. And if it doesn't like you it will run away!"

"Ding-dong-ding-dong!" said the clock suddenly, in a clear voice, making them all jump. It stopped walking when it chimed, but it ran after the children and Silky again at once. It was really a most extraordinary clock!

"Now we really must look for what *we* want,"

said Jo. "Are those hens over there, Bessie?"

"Yes, they are!" said Bessie. "Good! Come along and we'll get them. Oh, this is really a lovely land! I *am* glad we came! What fun it will be getting everything we want. I do wonder what Mother will say when we get home!"

XIX

MOON-FACE GETS INTO A FIX

The children went over to the hens that Jo had seen. They were lovely ones, but a very peculiar colour, for their wings were pale green and the rest of their feathers were buttercup yellow. They had funny high voices, and were very friendly indeed, for they came to press themselves round the children's legs like cats!

"Do you suppose Mother would like hens this colour?" said Jo doubtfully.

"I don't see why not," said Bessie. "I think they are very pretty. The thing is—do they lay good eggs?"

One of the hens at once laid an egg. It was large and quite an ordinary colour. Bessie was pleased.

"There you are!" she said. "If they lay eggs as big as this one, Mother will be *very* pleased. How many hens are there—one, two, three, four, five, six, seven! I wonder how we could take them all."

"Oh, they'll follow you," said Silky. "Just like

my clock follows me! Tell them you want them and they'll come."

"We want you to come with us, hens," said Jo at once, and the seven green-winged birds came over to him and lined up in a row to follow the children. It was really very funny.

"Well, that's our hens found!" said Bessie, pleased. "Now for the goat and the spade."

They wandered along, looking at everything. It didn't matter what any one wanted, they were sure to find it sooner or later! There were boats there, all kinds of dogs, shopping-baskets, rings, toys, work-baskets, and even such small things as thimbles!

"It's the strangest land I ever saw!" said Jo.

"We look pretty strange too!" said Fanny, giggling, as she looked round and saw the seven hens and the big clock padding along behind them. "Oh, look—there's the dearest, prettiest white goat I ever saw! Do let's take her!"

Sure enough, not far off was a lovely white nanny-goat, with soft brown eyes and perky ears. She looked quite ordinary except for two blue spots by her tail.

"Little white goat, come with us!" cried Fanny, and the goat trotted up at once. It took its place behind the hens, but it didn't seem to like the clock, which bumped into it every now and again, just to tease it.

"Don't do that, clock," said Silky.

"I hope your clock won't be a nuisance," said Bessie. "It's not behaving like a grandmother, is it?

It's a bit of a tease, *I* think."

"Now for the garden spade," said Jo, as he suddenly saw a fine strong spade hanging up on a fence with some other garden tools. "What about this one, girls? This looks strong enough for Father, doesn't it?"

He took it down and dug in the ground with it. It was a splendid spade. Jo put it over his shoulder, and the four of them grinned joyfully at each other.

"We've got everything we want," said Jo. "Come on. We'll go back to old Moon-Face and then we'll take some cakes for tea."

So, followed by the seven hens, the white goat, and the clock, the four of them made their way back to where they had left Moon-Face. But he

117

wasn't sitting where they had left him. He was pulling at a lovely rug, which was hanging from a tree. It was perfectly round, with a hole in the middle.

"Hallo, hallo!" yelled Moon-Face, as he saw them. "Look what I've got! Just what I've always wanted for my round tree-room—a round rug with a hole in the middle where the slippery-slip begins! Fine!"

"But, Moon-Face, you said you'd watch to see that the Land of Take-What-You-Want kept by the Faraway Tree all right, didn't you?" said Silky anxiously. "Where is the hole that leads down to the Tree?"

"Oh, it's somewhere over there," said Moon-Face, draping the rug round him and staggering off. "Come on. We're sure to find it."

But they didn't! It had gone—for the Land of Take-What-You-Want had moved away from the Faraway Tree.

"Moon-Face! It's too bad of you!" said Jo anxiously. "You did promise."

Moon-Face looked worried and pale. He hunted about for the hole—but there was no hole to be seen. He began to shake with fright.

"I've g-g-g-got you all into a t-t-terrible fix!" he said, in a trembling voice. "Here we are—stuck in a l-l-l-land where there's everything we w-w-w-want—and the only thing we w-w-w-want is to get away!"

Every one looked upset. This was too bad!

"I feel cross with you, Moon-Face," said Jo,

in a stern voice. "You said you'd keep guard and you didn't. I don't think you are much of a friend."

"And I'm ashamed of you too, Moon-Face," said Silky, who had tears in her eyes.

"We'll find some one to help us," said Moon-Face gloomily, and they all set off, followed by their hens, their goat, and the clock, which kept striking four o'clock, nobody knew why.

But now they found a very curious thing. There didn't seem to be any one at all in the Land of Take-What-You-Want! All the gnomes, the pixies, the brownies, and the elves had gone.

"They must have known the land was going to move off," said Moon-Face, with a groan. "And they all slipped down the ladder in time. Oh, why did I leave it?"

They wandered all over the land, which was not really very large, but was more crowded with things and animals than anywhere they had ever seen.

"I can't think what to *do*!" said Silky. "It's true that there is everything here we want—we shan't starve—but it isn't the sort of place we want to live in for ever!"

They walked here and there—and then suddenly they came to something they hadn't noticed before. It was a large and shining aeroplane!

"Ooooh!" said Jo, his eyes gleaming. "Look at that! How I wish I could fly an aeroplane! Can you fly one, Moon-Face?"

Moon-Face shook his head. Silky shook hers too. "That's no good then," said Jo, with a sigh.

"I thought perhaps we might fly away from this land in the aeroplane."

He climbed into the aeroplane and had a good look at it. There were five handles there. One had a label on that said "Up." Another had a label that said "Down." A third had one that said "Straight on," and a fourth and fifth said "To the Right" and "To the Left."

Jo stared at the handles in excitement. "I believe I could fly this aeroplane!" he said. "I do believe I could! It looks quite easy."

"No, Jo, don't," said Bessie, in alarm. But Jo had pressed the handle labelled "Up" and before any one could say another word the shining aeroplane had risen upwards with Jo, leaving the others staring open-mouthed on the ground below.

"Now Jo's gone!" said Fanny, and burst into tears. The aeroplane rose up and up. It circled round when Jo pressed the handle labelled "To the Right." It flew straight on when he pressed the third handle. And it flew down when he pressed the "Down" handle. It was just as easy as that!

Jo flew neatly down to the ground and landed not far away from the others. They rushed to him, shouting and laughing.

"Jo! Jo! Did you really fly it yourself?"

"Well, you saw me," said Jo, beaming at every one and feeling most tremendously grand. "It's quite easy. Get in, every one, and we'll fly off. Maybe we'll come to somewhere that Moon-Face knows, if we fly long enough!"

They all got in. Bessie packed the seven squawking hens at the back, and sat the white goat on her knee. The spade went on the floor. The clock made a nuisance of itself because it wouldn't stay where it was put, but kept climbing over everybody's feet to look out of the window. Silky began to wish she hadn't brought it.

"Ready?" asked Jo, pressing the handle marked "Up." And up they went! What a lovely feeling it was! They really couldn't help feeling excited.

Silky's clock got terribly excited too. It struck twenty-nine without stopping.

"I shan't wind you up to-night if you don't keep quiet," said Silky suddenly. And that finished the clock! It lay down in a corner and didn't say another ding or another dong!

"Where are we off to, I wonder?" said Bessie. But nobody knew!

XX

OFF TO DAME SLAP'S SCHOOL

Jo flew the aeroplane very well indeed. As soon as he was high enough he pressed the "STRAIGHT ON" handle, and the shining aeroplane flew forward.

The children leaned over the side to see what they were flying over. They had soon passed the Land of Take-What-You-Want, and came to a queer desolate country where no trees or grass grew, and not a house was to be seen.

"That's the Country of Loneliness," said Moon-Face, peering over. "Don't land there, Jo. Fly on."

Jo flew on. Once he came to an enormous hill, and he had to press the handle marked "UP" or the aeroplane would have flown straight into it. It was really great fun. Jo had had no idea that it was so easy to fly.

The little white goat on Bessie's knee was as good as gold. It licked Bessie's cheek every now and then just as if it were a dog! The hens were good and quiet, and the clock lay perfectly still.

The aeroplane flew over a land of great towers and castles. "Giantland!" said Silky, looking in wonder at the enormous buildings. "I hope we don't land here!"

"Rather not!" said Jo, and he pressed the "STRAIGHT ON" handle down still further, so that the aeroplane flew forward like a bird, faster and faster.

The children's hair streamed backwards, and as for Silky's mop of golden hair, it looked like a buttercup blown in the wind! Over the Land of Lollipop they went, and over the Country of Flop. And then the aeroplane began to make a funny noise!

"Hallo!" said Jo. "What's wrong?"

"I believe the aeroplane's tired," said Moon-Face. "It sounds out of breath."

"Don't be silly, Moon-Face," said Jo. "Aeroplanes don't get out of breath."

122

"This kind does," said Moon-Face. "Can't you hear it panting?"

It certainly seemed as if the aeroplane *was* panting! "Er-her — er-her — er-her!" it went.

"Had we better go down and give it a rest?" said Jo. "Yes," said Moon-Face, peering over the side. "It seems safe enough. I don't know what this land is, but it looks quite ordinary. There's a big green house down below with an enormous garden. Perhaps you could land on that long smooth lawn, Jo. We shouldn't get bumped then."

"Right," said Jo, and pressed the handle marked "DOWN." And down they went, gliding smoothly. Bump! They reached the grass and ran along on the aeroplane's big wheels. It stopped, and every one got out, glad to stretch their legs.

"Ten minutes' rest and the aeroplane will be ready to go off again," said Moon-Face, patting it.

"I wonder where we are," said Silky, looking round. Moon-Face gazed at the big green house in the distance — and then he frowned.

"Oh my!" he groaned. "I know whose house that is! It's a school, and it belongs to old Dame Slap! All the wicked pixies and gnomes and fairies are sent there to learn to be better! Let's hope Dame Slap doesn't catch sight of *us*!"

Every one looked about nervously — suddenly down a path came a tall old woman, with large spectacles on her long nose and a big white bonnet on her hair. Moon-Face ran to the aeroplane.

"Quick!" he said. "It's Dame Slap!"

But the old lady was up to them before they could escape. "Ah!" she said. "So here is another lot of naughty folk sent to me to cure! Come this way, please."

"We *haven't* been sent to you," said Jo. "We landed here to give our aeroplane a rest. We are on our way home."

"Naughty boy, to tell stories like that!" said Dame Slap, and she gave poor Jo a sharp smack that made him jump and turn red. "Come with me, all of you."

There didn't seem anything else to do. Jo, Bessie, Fanny, Moon-Face, Silky, the white goat, and the seven hens all followed Dame Slap, looking very miserable. The clock wouldn't walk, so Silky had to carry it.

Every one felt very hungry. Jo pulled Dame Slap's sleeve timidly. "Could we please have something to eat?" he asked.

"Tea will be ready in a few minutes," said Dame Slap. "Heads up, every one! Don't stoop, little girl!" The little girl was poor Fanny, who got a poke between her shoulders to make her stand up straight. Really, Dame Slap was not at all a nice person. It was very bad luck to have landed in her garden.

But everybody cheered up a little at the thought of tea. They were taken into a large hall, full of pixies and other fairy folk. They were all sitting down in rows at wooden tables, but they stood up when Dame Slap came into the room.

"Sit over there," said Dame Slap, pointing to an empty table. The children, Moon-Face, Silky, the goat, and the hens all took their places. The clock was stood at the end, and looked very sulky. The children looked down the tables. Oooh! What lovely buns! What gorgeous biscuits! What big jugs of lemonade!

Dame Slap ran her eyes over the little folk standing at the tables. She frowned. "Twinkle, come here!" she said. A small pixie walked up to her.

"Haven't I told you to brush your hair properly for meal-times?" said Dame Slap, and she slapped the pixie hard. Twinkle burst into tears.

"And there's Doodle over there with a torn tunic!" said Dame Slap. "Come here, Doodle."

Doodle came and was slapped very hard indeed. Bessie and Fanny felt nervous, and hoped that their hair and hands and dresses were clean and tidy.

"Sit!" said Dame Slap, and every one sat. "Have a bun?" said Jo, and passed Bessie and Fanny a plate of delicious-looking buns, with jam in the middle.

But what a shock for them! As soon as the buns touched their plates they turned into round hard pieces of stale bread! The children didn't dare to say a word. They saw that the same thing happened to every one in the room except Dame Slap, who made a marvellous tea of buns, biscuits, and pieces of plum cake.

The lemonade turned into water as soon as it

was poured into the glasses. It was dreadfully disappointing. In the middle of the meal a gnome-servant came in to say that some one wanted to speak to Dame Slap, and she went out of the room.

And then, dear me, the children found that the little folk in the room were decidedly very bad indeed! They crowded round them and poked them and pinched them, and made such rude remarks that Fanny began to cry.

They made such a noise that nobody heard Dame Slap coming back again! My goodness, wasn't she angry! She clapped her hands together and made every one jump nearly out of their skin!

"What's all this?" she shouted, in a very fierce voice. "Form up in a line! March past me at once!"

To the children's dismay every one got a good hard slap as they passed the cross old lady—but when they passed her she did not slap them, for she knew that they had been teased by the others. So they were very glad indeed, and felt a little more cheerful.

"Go to the schoolroom," said Dame Slap, when the last of the line had gone by. So to the schoolroom they all went and took their places, even the little green-winged hens.

"Now, please, answer the questions written on the blackboard," said Dame Slap. "You have each got paper and pencil. Any one putting down the wrong answers will be very sorry indeed."

Jo looked at the questions on the board. He read

them out to the others, in great astonishment.

"If you take away three caterpillars from one bush, how many gooseberries will there be left?"

"Add a pint of milk to a peck of peas and say what will be left over."

"If a train runs at six miles an hour and has to pass under four tunnels, put down what the guard's mother is likely to have for dinner on Sundays."

Everybody gazed at the board in despair. Whatever did the questions mean? They seemed to be nonsense.

"I can't do any," said Moon-Face, in a loud voice, and he threw down his pencil.

"It's all silly nonsense!" said Jo, and he threw down his pencil too. The girls did the same, and Silky tore her paper in half! All the pixie and fairy-folk stared at them in the greatest astonishment and horror.

"*In*deed!" said Dame Slap, suddenly looking twice as big as usual. "If that's how you feel, come with me!"

Nobody wanted to go with her—but they found that they had to, for their legs walked them after Dame Slap without being made to. It was most extraordinary. Dame Slap led them to a small room and pushed them all in. Then she shut the door with a slam and turned the key in the lock.

"You will stay there for three hours, and then I will come and see if you are sorry," she said.

"This is awful," said Jo gloomily. "She's no right to keep us here. We don't belong to her silly school. We haven't been naughty. It was just an accident that we came here."

"Well, what are we to do now?" said Silky, pushing back her golden hair. "It seems as if we'll have to stay here for three hours, and then say we're sorry and be slapped! I don't like it at all."

Nobody liked it. They all sat on the floor and looked angry and miserable. If only they could escape from Dame Slap's silly old school!

XXI

SILKY'S CLOCK IS VERY CLEVER

Jo sat hunched up near to Moon-Face. Silky and Bessie and Fanny talked together. The white goat sat on Bessie's knee and slept. The seven hens tried to scratch the hard floor, and clucked softly.

"Where's my clock?" said Silky suddenly.

Every one looked round the room for it. It wasn't there.

"It must have been left behind in the school-room," said Jo. "Never mind, Silky. You may get it back, if we get out of here in three hours' time."

"I hope so," said Silky. "It was a nice clock, and I liked it having feet to walk about on."

"It's lucky not to be locked up like us," said Jo gloomily. "If there was a window in this silly round room, we might break it and escape through that. But there isn't even a small window."

"And there isn't a fireplace either," said Moon-Face. "If there was we might squeeze up the chimney. Listen!" he said suddenly. "There's some one knocking at the door!"

They listened. Certainly there *was* some one outside, knocking gently.

"Come in, if you can!" said Moon-Face. "Unlock the door if the key's left in."

But the key wasn't left in! No, Dame Slap had taken that away, you may be sure!

"Who's there?" asked Silky.

"Ding-dong-ding-dong!" said a voice softly.

"It's my clock!" cried Silky excitedly. "It's come to join us!"

"Oooh!" said Moon-Face, his big face going red with joy. "Tell your clock to go and get the key from somewhere and let us out, Silky."

"That's no good," said Silky. "I noticed that Dame Slap wore all her keys on a string that hung from her waist. The clock could never get our key from her."

"Oh," said Moon-Face sadly. Everybody thought hard.

"Ding-dong-ding-dong!" said the clock outside, and knocked again.

"Look here, clock, it isn't a bit of good your dinging and donging and knocking to get in!" called Jo. "We are locked into this room, and we haven't got a key to get us out!"

"Dong!" said the clock dolefully. And then it

gave an excited "ding!" and began to dance about on its big feet, up and down, up and down, with its door wide open.

"Whatever is that clock doing?" said Silky, in astonishment.

"Warming its feet, I should think," said Fanny, with a giggle.

But it wasn't. It was jerking about trying to jolt its own key off the little hook inside it! And at last it managed it. Clang! The key fell to the ground.

"What*ever* is your clock doing?" said Jo to Silky. "It must have gone mad."

It hadn't. It was being very sensible. It kicked at the key with one of its feet—and the key slid under the door and into the room where the children were.

"Oooh, look!" said Moon-Face, in astonishment. "Your clock has jerked its key off the hook—and kicked it under the door, Silky. Really, it's a most peculiar clock!"

Jo snatched up the key. "It might fit the door!" he said. He tried it in the lock. It almost turned but not quite. He was dreadfully disappointed.

But Moon-Face grinned. He took the key and rubbed it with a little magic powder that he kept in a box in his pocket.

"Now try it," he said. So Jo slipped it into the lock once more—and it turned right round and unlocked the door!

They crowded quietly out of the room, Jo taking the clock's key with him. Silky gave the clock a hug and it said ding-dong quite loudly with joy!

"Sh!" said Silky. "Don't make a sound!"

"We'll try and find our aeroplane," said Jo. "Let's try to get out of a door into the garden. We shall soon find it then."

They tiptoed down a long passage—but just as they got to the end, who should they see coming along but old Dame Slap herself!

"Quick! Hide behind these curtains!" said Jo. They slipped behind them—but Dame Slap had heard something and came up to the curtains. She was just going to pull them apart when Silky's clock walked out, shouted "Ding-dong!" in her ear, and trod on her toes! Dame Slap gave a shout of rage and slapped the clock hard. It ran away down the passage, with Dame Slap after it.

"Good old clock!" said Silky joyfully. "It just walked out and ding-donged in time. Another minute and we would all have been found."

"Come on," said Moon-Face, peeping out of the curtains. "We'd better do our best to get into the garden now, whilst the old dame is out of the way."

They tiptoed down a long room and came to a door leading into the garden. Just as Jo was going to open it he pushed them all quickly back into the room.

"Dame Slap is coming in here!" he whispered. "Quick! Hide behind the furniture!"

So, quick as lightning, every one crouched down behind sofas and chairs, whilst Dame Slap opened the door and came in, grumbling. "Wait till I get that clock!"

And at that very moment the clock came running in on its flat feet and ding-donged very cheekily at her! Dame Slap picked up her skirts and tore down the long room and up the passage after it! The children and Moon-Face and Silky, the hens and the goats, rushed to the garden door, opened it and crowded out into the garden.

"Find the aeroplane, quick!" cried Jo. They ran down the path and looked for the shining aeroplane.

"There it is!" shouted Moon-Face, pointing to the aeroplane lying on the smooth grass. They all ran to it, and squeezed in.

"I don't like leaving my clock behind," said Silky. "It has been so clever. I wonder where it is."

"Look! There it is, with old Dame Slap after it!" cried Jo. Sure enough they saw the clock come waddling out from behind a bush, striking hard—and Dame Slap was after it, panting, and very red in the face.

The clock dodged neatly round a bush. Dame Slap tripped over a stone and fell down. The clock shot away to the aeroplane, and Silky helped it in. It sank down into a corner, and struck sixty-three times without stopping.

But this time nobody minded. They thought the clock was really quite a hero!

Dame Slap picked herself up and ran towards the aeroplane. Jo pressed down the "UP" handle. The propeller began to whirr round and round. The aeroplane quivered and shook. It rose gently into the air, and left Dame Slap below looking very angry indeed.

"Answer this question!" shouted Moon-Face, leaning overboard. "If five people, seven hens, one goat, and a clock go up in an aeroplane, put down how many slaps should be saved up for when they get home!"

Every one giggled.

"Do be careful where we land next time," said Bessie. "We really must get home soon."

"I think I know where we are now," said Moon-Face as they flew over a curious land where the trees were yellow and the grass was pink. "If you can fly straight on till you come to a silver tower — then to the right till you come to the Land of Sea-gulls — then to the left over the Three Bears' Wood — we shall soon be home!"

"Right!" said Jo. He watched out for the silver tower, and when he saw it, tall and gleaming, he pressed the handle marked "To THE RIGHT," and flew on till he came to the Land of Sea-gulls. This was quite easy to know, for all round and about, flying on snow-white wings, were hundreds of magnificent gulls. The aeroplane had to go slowly through the crowds of lovely birds. Jo flew to the left, and soon they were over the Three Bears' Wood, and saw the rose-covered cottage where Goldilocks lived with the bears.

"Good! Now it won't be long before we're home!" said Jo. He flew on till he came over the Enchanted Wood, and then landed in a field not far from it. Every one jumped out.

"That was a most exciting adventure," said Fanny. "But I hope we never see Dame Slap again!"

"Oh quick, catch the clock!" said Bessie. "It's trying to climb out of the aeroplane and it will fall!"

"Dong, dong, dong, dong!" said the clock, and it slid to the ground.

"We'll have to rush home now," said Jo, picking up his spade. "Good-bye, Silky; good-bye, Moon-Face. See you soon! Bessie, bring the goat, and Fanny and I will shoo the hens in front of us."

They left the aeroplane for Moon-Face and Silky to do what they liked with, and set off home.

And, dear me, *how* astonished their mother was to see the green-winged hens, the snow-white goat, and the fine garden spade!

"You must have been to the Enchanted Wood," she said.

"We've been *much* farther than that!" said Jo. And they certainly had, hadn't they?

XXII

UP TO TOYLAND

KNOCKITY-KNOCK-KNOCK
  Bang-bang-BANG!
  Rat-a-tatta-TAT!

"Good gracious! It sounds as if somebody's at the door!" said Jo. "I'll go and open it, Mother."

He went to open the door – and outside, looking very impatient, stood the old Saucepan Man. He was all hung about with pots and pans and kettles as usual, and had a saucepan for a hat.

"Hallo," said the Saucepan Man, "didn't you hear me knock? I've come to tell you that we must go to the top of the Faraway Tree to-morrow. There's a very nice land coming there."

"What is it?" asked Jo.

"Toyland," said Saucepan. "You could bring a

basket with you and collect quite a nice lot in time for Christmas."

"Oh what a good idea!" said Jo. He called to his two sisters. "Bessie! Fanny! Did you hear what the Saucepan Man said?"

"Yes!" they cried running to the door. "Oh, Saucepan, we really must come. Can we help ourselves to toys, do you suppose?"

"Well I've an aunt there," said Saucepan, "and if I tell her you're my friends, you can have what you want. Can you meet me at the top of the Faraway Tree to-morrow morning?"

"Oh, yes – and will Moon-Face and Silky be coming, too?" asked Bessie, joyfully. "We haven't seen them for ages."

"We'll have *fun*!" said Fanny.

"Yes, please," said Saucepan unexpectedly. "I'd like one very much."

"Like what?" said Bessie, astonished.

"What you just offered me – a bun," said Saucepan, looking round for it.

"Oh – you suddenly went deaf," said Bessie. "I just said – we'll have FUN."

"Oh! All the same I'd like a bun," said Saucepan. He often went deaf and heard things wrong, because his saucepans and kettles made such a noise as he walked about, that he found it quite difficult to hear properly.

Jo got him a bun out of the cake-tin. He went off, munching happily, his pans rattling and clanging round him. "See you to-morrow!" he called.

The next day the three children set off to the

Faraway Tree. Into the dark Enchanted Wood they went, and followed the winding path they knew so well. The trees whispered round them as they went. They always seemed to have secrets to tell one another. "Wisha-wisha-wisha," they whispered.

They came to the Faraway Tree in the middle of the wood. It looked even more enormous than usual. It towered up to the clouds, and the children couldn't even see the top of it. Its trunk was so big that it was quite a walk to go all the way round it!

"Hurrah! The tree's growing blackberries today," said Jo, picking some big ripe ones.

"Well, it shouldn't, then," said Bessie.

"Blackberries grow on bushes, not on trees. The Faraway Tree's made a mistake!"

They began to climb the tree. A little way up it stopped growing blackberries and grew pine-cones!

"Not so good," said Jo. "We can't eat pine-cones, Faraway Tree."

"It's a very *exciting* tree, this," said Fanny. "Always growing different things all the way up – and having people living in it too – and a slippery-slide all the way inside from the top to the bottom. I'm glad we live near a tree like this. We're lucky."

"Yes. I bet a lot of children wish they lived near it too," said Jo, helping Bessie over a steep bit. "My word, the adventures we've had!"

"Look out – I can hear Dame Washalot's dirty water coming down!" yelled Fanny suddenly.

And, sure enough, down came a cascade of soapy water, running down the trunk, splashing on the boughs, and soaking a little pixie who was sitting nearby.

"Bother!" she said. "And I brought an umbrella with me too, in case I didn't hear the water coming!"

Jo laughed. "I should put on a bathing-suit next time and not bother about an umbrella," he said. "Anyway, the sun will soon dry you!"

They went up, passing little windows in the Faraway Tree, and came to Silky's small yellow door. They knocked, but there was no answer.

"She's gone up to the top of the tree, I expect," said Jo. "Come on – we don't want to keep the others waiting."

They climbed right up to Moon-Face's little door. From inside came the sound of chattering, and the noise of jangling and clanging.

"The Saucepan Man's there all right," said Jo. "And the others, too I should think." He banged on the door. Moon-Face opened it, beaming all over his big round face. "Oh, come in," he said. "We're just having a snack before we go."

"What sort of snack?" asked Bessie, going in with the others. "Pop biscuits? I love those."

"No – something Saucepan bought when he was in the Land of Surprises," said Moon-Face. "Well-I-Never Rolls."

"What a peculiar name," said Jo, looking at the dish of nice crusty little rolls. "What do they taste of?"

"Try one," said Moon-Face. "And tell us!"

Jo took a roll and bit into it. "Tastes of cheese," he said. "No – well I never, it tastes of ginger now. No, it doesn't – it's chocolate! And now it tastes of coconut – and it's got bits of coconut in it – no, they've gone – it's treacly now. Well I never!"

"Yes. Most peculiar, isn't it?" said Moon-Face. "No wonder they're called Well-I-Never Rolls. You just simply never know what they'll taste of next. Every chew you have tastes of something different."

"Jolly good," said Jo. "I'll have another. My – this tastes of pickled onions – no, it doesn't – it's custard – lovely!"

"Mustard," said Saucepan in disgust. "I'd hate one to taste of mustard."

"I said CUSTARD," said Jo, and then made a face. "Oh my word, it *is* mustard now. Horrible!"

"Just what I said. Mustard," said Saucepan. He bit into his. "Ah – mint! Delicious! Why, it's mint sauce, I can taste the tiny bits of mint."

"You'll find you've got lamb next," said Silky.

Saucepan looked surprised. "No – it isn't ham," he said.

"I said LAMB!" shouted Silky.

"No, it's not jam," said Saucepan. "Dear me – it's lamb! Lamb and mint sauce – how clever! Really these rolls are remarkable."

So they were. The six of them finished up the whole dish of them. "I wish I'd brought heaps more," said Saucepan, getting up. "Well, aren't we going up to Toyland? Do hurry up."

They were all ready. They went out of Moon-Face's little round room and climbed up the topmost branch into a cloud. They came to the little yellow ladder that led upwards through the last bit of cloud. Toyland should be at the top!

Saucepan went first. He climbed off the topmost rung of the ladder, and called down to the others.

"Yes, it's here. Come on!"

Up they all went, and at last stood in Toyland. But there seemed to be no toys about at all. Saucepan pointed to a town not far off. Flags were flying gaily from little houses.

"There's the Village of Toys," he said. "Now we'll go and find my aunt."

They set off to the village. But when they got there, Saucepan stopped and looked puzzled.

"Dear me," he said, "this isn't the Land I hoped. The toys are all alive – look, isn't that a Teddy Bear walking about?"

"Yes," said Bessie. "Good gracious – we can't take toys like these away to play with at home! They're as big as we are!"

"I'll find my aunt," said Saucepan, and they all walked down the village street, meeting three or four sailor dolls, a curious man who had no legs but just wobbled along, and some pretty little dolls.

Saucepan's aunt was nowhere to be found. She kept a toyshop, and, of course, there was no toyshop there, because the toys lived in little houses made of coloured wooden bricks.

"Your aunt lives in the other land, you silly," said Silky. "This must be the Land of Toys, not Toyland."

"Oh, well – let's enjoy ourselves, anyway," said Saucepan. "Here comes another Wobbly Man. Let's try and push him over."

The Wobbly Man was astonished and annoyed

when Saucepan gave him a punch. He wobbled over backwards and then came forwards again, only to get another punch, this time from Moon-Face.

"How dare you?" cried the Wobbly Man in a rage. "That's not the way for visitors to behave! I'll report you to the Captain of the Soldiers!"

He wobbled off at a remarkable speed. The three children and Silky felt a bit scared.

"You shouldn't go round punching people, Saucepan," said Jo. "Not even to see them wobble. I do hope we shan't get into trouble."

Saucepan suddenly went deaf and didn't hear. He hardly ever did hear when somebody scolded him. "Look, there's a clockwork mouse running along!" he said, pointing. "Run, mouse, run! Meow! MEOW!"

The clockwork mouse was very frightened when it heard Saucepan mewing. It turned and ran off at top speed, almost bumping into a toy soldier.

"Look – there's the Captain of the Soldiers," said Bessie, afraid. "And the Wobbly Man is with him. He's complained of us, as he said he would. We'd better run away."

"No," said Jo. "We can easily explain, and Saucepan must say he's sorry."

Up marched the soldier, clickety-click, as smart as could be. He saluted – click!

"You must come with me," said the Captain, in a most commanding voice. "You are not toys, and should not be here. Also your behaviour must be looked into. Follow me, quick MARCH!"

"We'd better follow," said Jo. "He can't do

anything to us; he's only a toy, even if he *is* alive.
And I must say I'd rather like to see what that toy
fortress is like inside."

So they all followed the soldier and the Wobbly
Man. Whatever was going to happen?

XXIII
THEY GET INTO TROUBLE

The Captain took them through the village and up
to the wooden fortress. It was very like a toy fortress
that Jo had once had. It even had a wooden
drawbridge that could be pulled up or let down.

It was let down for them to walk over. Guns
stood here and there. Jo went up to one. "Funny
old gun!" he said. "Look there's a knob to pull back
and then let go, just like the toy cannon I had in my
little fortress at home."

He pulled back the knob, let it go and then
BANG! The gun went off with a most tremendous
noise! The Wobbly Man was so shocked that he
almost fell over, and it took a lot of wobbles for him
to stand upright again.

The toys in the village below were so frightened
when the gun went BANG that they tore out of
their little houses and ran for their lives! The
Captain was very angry indeed.

"Now see what you've done!" he said to Jo. "Let
off the gun, and scared everybody! You must be
mad."

142

"I'm very sorry," said poor Jo. "I never thought the gun would go off like that."

"Well what did you think it would do?" said the Captain, in a rage. "Whistle a tune or dance a jig?"

Nobody dared to laugh. The Captain led them on again, and soon they came to a door that led into a wooden tower. They went in and found themselves in a room with a table and a chair at one end, and nothing else.

The Captain sat himself down in the chair. "Stand up straight," he said. Everyone stood up very straight, even Saucepan.

"Salute," said the Captain, and everyone saluted, though Moon-Face used the wrong hand.

"Dismiss!" said the Captain, and everyone stared. What did he mean?

"No – that's wrong," said the Captain. "Don't dismiss. Stand at ease."

They obeyed. The Captain rapped loudly on the table. "You are accused of not being toys. You are accused of punching Wobbly Men. You are accused of setting off guns. You – "

"Only *one* Wobbly Man, and *one* gun," said Jo. "We're sorry and we won't do it again. We'll dismiss now!"

But before they could go they heard the noise of marching feet, and into the room came about fifty soldiers, all very wooden. They surrounded the children and the others.

"To the deepest dungeon with them!" ordered the Captain.

"NO!" shouted Jo, and he pushed the nearest

soldier hard. The soldier fell against the man next to him and knocked him over. That one fell against the next one and he went down, too, knocking the soldier next to him – and before five seconds had passed every soldier was lying flat on the floor.

"It's like when we put dominoes in a row – knock the first over, and down goes the whole row!" said Fanny with a giggle.

The Captain looked most alarmed. What was he to do with people like these? Good gracious – one push, and all his men were down!

He banged on the table. "Order! Order! Get up! Do you think you are skittles, men?"

The men got up, but not one of them would go near the little group of six prisoners.

"Now listen," said the Captain. "Either you become toys, or you go to the deepest dungeon. You can choose."

"All right – we'll be toys, then!" said Jo with a grin. "I'll be a clockwork clown, and go head-over-heels all the time!"

He began to go head-over-heels all round the room, and knocked into one of the soldiers. Down they all went again, like a row of skittles!

"Right – you're a clockwork clown," said the Captain. "What will *you* be?" and he pointed at Moon-Face.

"A teddy bear," grinned Moon-Face, "with a growl in my middle." And he pressed himself in the middle and pretended to growl.

"I'll be a pretty doll," said Silky, and began to walk about stiffly like a doll.

"And I'll be a furry grey rabbit!" said the Saucepan Man. "I'll grow long floppy ears and grey fur!"

"We'll be dolls," said Bessie and Fanny together, and they walked about stiffly like Silky, giggling all the time.

"Right," said the Captain thankfully. "You are now toys, and can remain in Toyland. Dis-MISS!"

The six of them went out laughing, Jo still turning head-over-heels, just for fun. They went over the drawbridge and into the town. In the distance they saw an enormous Noah's Ark.

"Let's go and see the animals coming out two by two," said Bessie, and they set off.

Fanny was just going to say something to Saucepan, who was in front of her, when she stopped. She stared hard.

She saw something really very peculiar. Saucepan wore a saucepan for a hat, as usual – but, dear me, he had suddenly grown two huge floppy ears! The saucepan sat on top, looking rather queer.

"Saucepan," said Fanny, astonished. "Saucepan, what's wrong with you?"

Saucepan turned round, surprised, and everyone got a tremendous shock. His face was covered in grey fur and he had very long whiskers!

"He's a toy rabbit!" said Fanny, with a squeal. "Saucepan – you're a toy rabbit! You said you would be, and now you are."

They were all most astonished. They stared and stared at poor Saucepan. How queer to see his face all grey, topped with two floppy ears and long quivering whiskers!

Saucepan looked at himself in one of his bright pans, which he used as a looking glass. He was shocked to see such a grey face looking back at him. He gazed round at the others, scared.

Then he gave a shout and pointed to Jo. "Well! Look at *him*! He's a clockwork clown now, hat and all! Yes, and he's got a key in his back! Jo, you're a clown! No wonder you keep going head-over-heels!"

Jo turned another somersault at once. The others gazed at him. Yes, Jo was a clown, with a clown's hat and dress. His face was daubed in red and white like a clown's, too.

Fanny looked at the others, and squealed again. "Look at Moon-Face – he's a fat, round little teddy bear, with a round, teddy bear face that's hardly like Moon-Face's at all! Oh, Moon-Face – is it really you?"

"Yes," said Moon-Face, putting up his hand to feel his face. "Oh dear – I've gone all furry. Where are my clothes? They've gone."

Jo pressed him in the middle and a most alarming growl came out – grrrrrrrrr!

"Don't," said Silky. "You made me jump. Don't press him again, Jo. Oh, I say – this is dreadful. We're all toys. Look at *me*!"

"You're not so bad," said Jo, looking at her. "You are just about the prettiest little doll I ever saw. And Bessie and Fanny are dolls, too. Look at them walking about, as stiff as can be. Bessie, can you sit down?"

"Not very easily," said Bessie, trying to sit on a

146

nearby wall. "I can't seem to bend. And I can't shut my eyes, either."

"Perhaps they will shut when you lie down," said Moon-Face, speaking in a funny growly voice.

So Bessie lay down on some grass for a moment and at once her eyes shut!

"Yes. We're *really* toys," said Fanny. "It must have begun happening when we said we'd be toys, and chose what we'd be. But we only said it for fun."

"I know. But you never know what will happen in the Lands that come to the top of the Faraway Tree," groaned Jo. "Moon-Face, will we stop being toys when we get out of this Land?"

"No, I don't think so," said the teddy bear. "And anyway, how do you think you are going to head-over-heels down the Faraway Tree? We'll just have to hope this will all wear off."

"I don't like being a toy rabbit," said Saucepan mournfully. "I feel silly. Do you suppose my face will come my own again if I wash it?"

"No," said Jo, turning head-over-heels for about the fiftieth time; "toy rabbits always stay furry. It's your ears that look so funny with that saucepan stuck on top of them. Why don't you take it off?"

"Well, I should get a cold," said Saucepan. "I always wear a hat. I don't feel right without a saucepan for a hat."

"You certainly don't *look* right now," said Moon-Face, in his growly voice.

"Nor do you," said Saucepan. "I wish you'd look like Moon-Face again. I don't like you like that."

"Oh, come on," said Jo, going head-over-heels

again. "Let's explore Toy Village and hope all this wears off. If only I didn't have to go head-over-heels so often! I'm getting very tired of it."

"So are we," said Fanny, getting out of his way. "Do keep over there, Jo – you'll knock me over."

The little company went on through Toy Village. Nobody took much notice of them now because they looked exactly like toys. Wobbly men wobbled about, looking very busy, and teddy bears lazed around, fat and cheerful looking. Dolls of all kinds went here and there, and they saw the little clockwork mouse again.

"Meow!" said Saucepan, and it fled.

"You're unkind to it," said Fanny. "It's a dear little thing. Oh, dear – I do feel funny, walking stiffly like this. I'm sure I couldn't run, even if I had to!"

"Look, here come the Noah's Ark Animals," said Jo, getting up from another somersault. "Two by two, just as they ought to. Two lions, two bears, two rabbits . . . "

"Two ducks, two mice," went on Fanny.

"MEOW!" said Saucepan at once again. "Meow!"

But the Noah's Ark mice took no notice of him. However somebody else did! Behind the mice were two cats, and one of them left the row of animals and came over to Saucepan, glaring at him.

"What did you just say then?" said the wooden cat.

"Meow," said Saucepan, "meow, meow, meow!"

"How dare you call me such rude names!" said

the cat, and showed claws in her wooden paws. Saucepan backed away hurriedly.

"I didn't mean to call you names," he said. "I just said, 'meow, meow, meow,' to the mice."

"Well, that means, 'You're a very ugly cat with a crooked tail!' " said the cat angrily. "My tail is *not* crooked. Don't use cat-language if you don't know what it means!"

"Get back into line, cat!" called Mr Noah, and the cat obeyed. Saucepan was very thankful. Dear, dear – to think those simple meows had meant all that in cat-language! He really must be careful.

"Let's go on," he said to the others, who were as surprised as he was. "Old Moon-Face might suddenly begin to growl, and goodness knows what that might mean in bear-language! We don't want those two white bears and the two brown ones to come after us."

"Well, let's go another way," said Jo, gloomily turning another somersault. "Blow this head-over-heels business. I'm tired of it!"

They turned down another way. Oh, dear – was this strange spell wearing off yet? It didn't seem like it!

XXIV
MR OOM-BOOM-BOOM

They came to a little garage. A very furry rabbit was busy putting petrol into a car driven by another toy rabbit. They looked at Saucepan in surprise as he came along with the others.

"Hallo!" said the garage rabbit. "What's the idea of wearing a saucepan for a hat? I can't say I've ever seen a rabbit wearing a hat before."

"Well, you've seen one now," said Saucepan, not very politely. "Bother these awful floppy ears. I hate them. They make me look like a toy rabbit."

"Well – but you *are* a toy rabbit, floppy ears and all," said the rabbit, staring.

"That's where you're wrong," said Saucepan. "I'm not. I hate being one. Ugly creatures, with stupid long ears and quivering whiskers!"

"Stop it, Saucepan," said Jo, warningly. He turned to the surprised rabbit.

"You must excuse him," he said; "he's really a Saucepan Man, as you can see. And I'm not really a clockwork clown, I'm a boy. Oh – excuse me, I can feel another somersault coming on!"

He turned head-over-heels and then stood up straight again.

"I see," said the rabbit. "Well, I should just hate to be an ugly little Saucepan Man, so I know what he feels about being a rabbit – though rabbits are very handsome creatures – like myself. He ought to be pleased he's turned into one."

"Well, we really like being ourselves best," said Fanny. "I'm a little girl, not a doll. And this teddy bear is really Moon-Face."

"Never heard of him," said the rabbit. "Didn't know there were such things as Moon-Faces."

Fanny giggled. Silky went up to the rabbit and

smiled at him. "Please do help us," she said.

The rabbit stared at her. He thought she was the very prettiest little doll he had ever seen in Toy Village. The rabbit who was inside the car leaned out.

"Of course we'll help you," he said. "What do you want us to do?"

"Well, we did hope all this would wear off," said Silky in a high little doll's voice that sounded rather sweet. "But it hasn't. And we wondered if you knew how we could get back into ourselves again."

The two rabbits looked at one another. "Difficult," said one. "Very," said the other.

"What about the old Spell-Maker, Mr Oom-Boom-Boom?" said the first one. "If he's in a good temper, he might do something for them."

"Yes. But if he's in a bad temper, he might turn them into something worse," said the second rabbit.

"Then we won't go there," said Jo hurriedly, and turned another somersault.

"We could see if he's in a good or bad temper before we say anything," said the rabbit. "I'll take you there in my car, if you can all squeeze in."

"Well – we might try," said Moon-Face, his little round teddy bear face looking worried.

The rabbit made Silky sit next to him. He thought she was really beautiful, and very sweet. "I am sure, if *you* went to ask Mr Oom-Boom-Boom a favour he would say 'yes' at once," he said. "I never saw anyone quite so pretty as you."

"Well you're a very handsome rabbit," said Silky, and that pleased him very much. They all squeezed into the car somehow, waved to the friendly garage rabbit, and set off.

"I feel a somersault coming on," said Jo suddenly. "I'm so sorry – but will you please stop the car so that I can get out and turn head-over-heels?"

"You're going to be a bit of a nuisance," said the rabbit driver. "Can't you do about a dozen, and make those do for a while?"

"I'll try," said poor Jo. So he got out and did nine, but no more would come, so he got back into the car. "I do wish you didn't wear so many pans and kettles," he said to Saucepan. "Move that kettle, will you? It's sticking its spout into me."

"Kettles don't have snouts," said Saucepan.

"SPOUT, I said, not Snout," said Jo crossly. "Now there's something else sticking into me – a saucepan handle."

"I haven't got any candles," said Saucepan, mishearing again. "You know I haven't. You're just making a fuss, with all your chatter about snouts and candles."

"I said SHOUTS and PANDLES," bawled Jo, losing his temper. "No, I don't mean that – I mean, I mean . . . "

"Pouts and Scandles," said Fanny with a squeal of laughter. "Be quiet, you two. Saucepan, dear, be sensible. He meant Spouts and Handles – look, they're sticking into him."

"Well, why didn't he say so then," grumbled Saucepan, moving the kettle and the saucepan and sticking them into Moon-Face instead. "Goodness, Moon-Face, what are *you* growling about now?"

Moon-Face turned his teddy bear face to Saucepan. "You're not kind," he said.

"No, I don't mind," said Saucepan, whose hearing had gone quite wrong with the noise of the car and the jangling of his pans. "Of course I don't mind. Why should I mind? Mind what, anyhow?"

"Stop talking," said the rabbit at the wheel. "I keep listening and it all sounds so mad that I'm sure I shall drive into a tree or something. Anyway, I want to talk to this dear little Silky doll here."

Nobody talked after that except Silky and the toy rabbit. The car went on and on, and at last Jo wanted to get out and go head-over-heels again. "Can you stop?" he called.

"Good gracious me, I've gone right past Mr Oom-Boom-Boom!" said the rabbit, putting on the brake so suddenly that the saucepan flew off Saucepan's head and rolled away down the road. "Yes, get out and somersault for a bit while I turn the car round."

So Jo turned about ten somersaults, while the toy rabbit turned the car round again. Then back they went to find Mr Oom-Boom-Boom.

"Don't start talking to Silky or you'll go right past again," begged Fanny. But this time the rabbit kept an eye open for Mr Oom-Boom-Boom's house and suddenly put on the brakes again.

"There goes another of my saucepans," groaned Saucepan. "Do we *have* to stop so suddenly?"

Nobody took any notice of him. They stared at a funny little door set in a grassy hill. On it was printed in bold black letters:

OOM-BOOM-BOOM. KNOCK SEVEN
TIMES.

"Silky, you go," said Fanny. "Perhaps Oom-
Boom-Boom will be nice to you. You really do look
very sweet."

"All right. I'll knock," said Silky bravely, though
she felt very scared. She got out of the car, and
went up to the little door. She took hold of the
knocker and knocked seven times – blam-blam-
blam-blam-blam-blam-blam!

A loud voice came from inside. "Stop knocking.
Once is quite enough!"

"Oh dear – he's in a bad temper!" called the
rabbit. "Come back quickly, Silky, and we'll drive
off."

"I can't come," wailed Silky. "The knocker has
got hold of my hand. It won't let go!"

Jo jumped out at once and went to her help. But
Silky was quite right. The knocker had fast hold of
her hand and wouldn't let it go.

Moon-Face went to help, too, and then the
Saucepan Man, looking very worried. And just at
that very moment the door opened, pulling poor
Silky with it, and a voice boomed out loudly:

"WHAT'S ALL THIS? DISTURBING ME IN
THE MIDDLE OF MY SPELLS!"

Everyone thought that Oom-Boom-Boom was a
very good name for him, booming at them like
that. But he wasn't a bit like his voice. He was an
old brownie with a beard so long that it trailed
behind him. He had big, pointed ears, and wore a

154

funny little round hat with feelers on it like a butterfly's. His eyes were as green as grass and very bright indeed.

He frowned at them all – and then he saw Silky, still held by the knocker.

"Ah," he said, and a smile broke over his face like the sun shining out suddenly. "Ah! What a dear little doll! No wonder my knocker wouldn't let you go. Where did you come from? I've never seen a doll as pretty as you! Do you know where you ought to be?"

"No," said Silky, with a gasp.

"You ought to be standing at the very top of the great big Christmas Tree that Santa Claus has in his castle!" said Oom-Boom-Boom in his booming voice. "He's always looking for the prettiest doll in the world to put there, but he's never found one as pretty as you yet!"

"I'm not a doll," said Silky. "I'm a pixie. I've been turned into a doll to-day."

"Let her go, knocker," said the brownie. "Come in, all of you. Why have you paid me this visit?"

"He seems in a very good temper now," whispered Jo to Moon-Face. "I think it's safe to go in."

They all went in and the door shut with a bang that made them jump. Inside there was a narrow, very winding passage that led into the hill. They followed the brownie down it, everybody stumbling over his very long beard that trailed out behind him. He didn't seem to mind.

He took them to a big room with a very low ceiling. A great fire burned in the middle, but the flames

155

were green, not red, and no heat came from them.

"I was just making a few spells," said Oom-Boom-Boom, his big voice echoing all round the room. "I'm a spell-maker, you know."

"Yes. That's why we came," said Silky, feeling very nervous. "Please, dear Mr Oom-Boom-Boom, will you use a spell to help us? We want to go back to our right selves. I'm a pixie, really, as I told you."

"And we're really little girls," said Bessie and Fanny. "And this clown is a boy, and the toy rabbit is old Saucepan Man . . . "

"And I'm Moon-Face," said Moon-Face, his little teddy bear face looking very earnest. "Please do help us."

"Ha," said Oom-Boom-Boom, looking round at them and beaming, "well, I don't mind doing that. That's easy. But I'll do it on one condition."

"What's that?" asked Jo, his heart sinking.

"I'll turn five of you back to your own shapes – but I want this little doll here, the very pretty one, to stay with me so that I can sell her to Santa Claus to put on the top of his Christmas Tree! It will be such an honour for her. You'd love that, wouldn't you, my pretty dear?" he said to Silky, turning to her.

Silky looked very frightened. "Well – I'll stay and let you sell me to Santa Claus," she said, "if you will use a spell on the others."

"Oh, dear, darling Silky!" said Moon-Face, putting his furry arm round her, "how sweet you are! But we wouldn't let you. We'd never leave you here alone."

156

"Never," said Jo. "NEVER!"

"Never, never, never, never," said Jo, Bessie and Fanny.

"I'm going to stay," said Silky, looking as if she was going to cry, but smiling at them all the same. "It won't be so bad, going to Santa Claus, though it sounds very dull standing on the top of his Christmas Tree. But it's for you, you see, so I want to do it!"

"Of course she wants to do it," said Oom-Boom-Boom. "She's a sensible little doll."

"Be quiet," said Jo. "I tell you we won't let her do it! We'd rather be toys all our lives long than that!"

Then Mr Oom-Boom-Boom lost his temper. He rushed at Jo – but Jo did a very clever thing. He caught him by his very long beard, dragged him to a big table and tied him to it with his beard, making dozens of knots!

"Now, quick, let's go!" he cried. "Sorry about tying you up, Oom-Boom-Boom, but you're not going to have Silky. Run everyone!"

They ran up the winding passage and came out on the hillside. And oh, joy, there was the rabbit waiting in his car! What a wonderful sight!

XXV
IN SANTA CLAUS' CASTLE

Jo got to the car first. "Quick!" he cried. "I can hear Oom-Boom-Boom coming! He must have got free."

So he had! He appeared at the door of his queer house, and they saw that he had freed himself by cutting his beard short. He did look queer.

The toy rabbit revved up his car and it shot off, almost before Saucepan was safely in. A kettle flew, clanging, down the road, and Saucepan groaned.

"Well, thank goodness that kettle's gone," said Jo. "It can't stick into me again. Oh, dear – I feel I want to turn head-over-heels."

"Well, you can't," said Moon-Face firmly. "Unless you want to be caught by the Oom-Boom-Boom fellow. Here, Saucepan, hang on to Jo, and stop him turning head-over-heels in the car!"

It was difficult to stop him, but they managed it. After they had gone a good way the rabbit stopped the car for a talk, and Jo took the chance of turning about a dozen somersaults.

"You know, *I* think you ought to go to the Land of Santa Claus," said the rabbit. "I do really. Not to give him Silky, of course, that would never do – but to tell him you aren't toys and to ask him if he can stop you being what you aren't."

"That's a bit muddling," said Moon-Face, trying to work it out. "Yes – it seems a good idea. After all, he deals in toys, doesn't he? He must know them very well. He'll be able to tell we're not real toys, and *might* help us."

"We know he's kind," said Silky. "He's so fond of children. Let's go to him. How can we get there, though? This Land may stay at the top of the Faraway Tree for some time – and the Land of

Santa Claus may not be the next one to arrive."

"That's true enough," said the rabbit. "Actually the next Land on the timetable is the Land of Squalls, which doesn't sound too good. But I'll tell you what I can do for you!"

"What!" asked Jo.

"I can drive you to the next station and put you on a train for the Land of Santa Claus," said the toy rabbit. "I happened to notice that some trains there do go to his Land. What about it, friends?"

"A very good idea," said everyone, and off they went. They came to a funny little station after a while, and they all got out.

"I wish you could stay in my Land for ever, little Silky doll," said the rabbit to Silky. "You really are the prettiest thing I ever saw. But there – you'd be unhappy and I couldn't bear that."

"I'll write to you," said Silky.

"Will you really?" said the rabbit. "Do you know, I've never had a letter in my life! It *would* make me feel important! Look, there's a train in!"

"I say! This train's going to the Land of Santa Claus! What a bit of luck!" cried Moon-Face. "Good-bye, Rabbit. You really have been a good friend. I'll write to you."

"My word – fancy me getting *two* letters!" said the delighted rabbit.

"We'll *all* write," said Jo, shaking his furry hand warmly. "Good-bye. It's been lovely meeting you."

Silky gave him a kiss and he nearly cried for joy. "I've never been kissed before," he said. "Never. A kiss – and letters – my word, I *am* a lucky rabbit!"

They all climbed into the train and waved good-bye.

"Nice fellow, that rabbit," said Jo. "Well, we're off again. I wonder how far it is."

It was quite a long way, and they all fell asleep. A porter wakened them up at last. "Hey, you! Don't you want to get out here?" he said. "This is where toys usually get out."

They scrambled out because the station board said, "Get out here for the Castle of Santa Claus!"

"Just in time," said Jo, yawning. "Oh, my – here I go, turning head-over-heels again!"

"There's the castle – look!" said Bessie, pointing to a magnificent castle with many towers, rising high on a hill nearby. "And, goodness – look at the snow! Anyone would think it was winter here."

"Oh, it always is," said the porter. "It wouldn't be much good for sleighs, would it, if there wasn't snow? Is Santa Claus expecting you? His sleigh usually meets the train in case there are any visitors for him."

"Is that it down there?" asked Moon-Face, pointing down into the snowy station yard. A sleigh was there, with four fine reindeer, whose bells jingled as they moved restlessly. A small red imp held the reins.

"Yes, that's the sleigh. Better go and get in," said the porter. He stared hard at Silky. "I say – isn't that a pretty doll? I bet Santa Claus will want her for his own Christmas Tree."

They went to the sleigh and got into it. "To Santa Claus, please," said Jo, and off they went, gliding smoothly over the snow, drawn by the four eager reindeer.

They arrived at the castle. They felt rather nervous when they saw how big and grand it was. They stood at an enormous door, carved with all kinds of toys, and rang a great bell.

The door swung open. "Please come in," said a teddy bear, dressed just like a footman. "Santa Claus will see you in a few minutes."

They went into a big hall and then into a great room, where many little imps and goblins were at work. "You might like to look round while you're waiting," said the bear footman. "You'll see the imps painting the dolls' houses, and the goblins putting growls into us bears, and you'll see how the somersaults are put into the clockwork clowns."

"I don't want to see that," said Jo, feeling at once that he wanted to go head-over-heels. He turned a few and then stood up again. "What are those imps doing over there?" he said.

"Putting the hum into tops," said the footman. "But don't go too near. One of the hums might get into you by mistake, and that's *such* a nuisance, you know!"

They stood at a safe distance, watching. It was very interesting indeed. So many things were going on; there was so much to see and hear, that they almost forgot they were toys themselves.

"How's your growl, bear?" said a little imp, running up to Moon-Face. He punched him in the middle and Moon-Face growled deeply. "Grrrrrr!

Leave me alone! I don't like people doing that. Grrrrrrr!"

"Look – oh, look – isn't that Santa Claus himself?" cried Bessie, suddenly, as a big man came into the room dressed in bright red. He wore a hood trimmed with white, and his jolly face had eyes that twinkled brightly.

"Yes. It's Santa Claus!" cried Jo. Santa Claus heard him and came over at once. He looked in surprise at Silky.

"Why!" he said, "where did you come from? *You* weren't made in my castle, by imps and goblins. You are the loveliest doll I've ever seen. I've a good mind to keep you for myself and put you at the very top of my own big Christmas Tree."

"No, no, please not!" said Silky. Santa Claus looked down at the others. He seemed puzzled.

"Where do you all come from?" he said. "I am quite sure I have never had any toys made like you. The rabbit, dressed up in kettles and saucepans, for instance – and this funny little bear. He doesn't seem like a proper teddy."

"We're *not* proper toys!" said Bessie. "Santa Claus, we got turned into toys in the Castle of the Toy Soldiers. I'm a little girl, really."

"And I'm Moon-Face, who lives at the top of the Faraway Tree," said Moon-Face.

"What! The famous Moon-Face, who has a slippery-slip in his room, going down the tree from the top to the bottom!" cried Santa Claus. "My word – I've often wanted to see that! Do you think I'm too fat to go down it?"

"No – no, I don't think so," said Moon-Face, looking at him. "I could give you *two* cushions to sit on instead of one. Sir, if you'd like to come now, you can go up and down the Faraway Tree as often as you like – we'll haul you up in the washing-basket every time you arrive at the bottom, and you can slide down again from the top!"

"Let's go now," said Santa Claus in delight. "Well, well – to think I'm meeting the famous Moon-Face at last! And I suppose this darling doll is Silky the pixie. And of course – this is the old Saucepan Man!"

"But – how do you know us?" asked Moon-Face, astonished.

"Oh, I've heard about you from the children," said Santa Claus. "They keep asking me for books about you, to go into their Christmas stockings and they looked so exciting that I read them all. I *did* want to meet you!"

Well, wasn't that a bit of luck? Santa Claus called his sleigh and they all got in. "To the top of the Faraway Tree," commanded Santa Claus, and away they went. It didn't take very long. In quite a little while the sleigh landed on a broad bough near the top of the tree, and they all got out.

"My room is just a bit higher up," said Moon-Face, and led the way. They were soon in his little round room. He pointed to the curious hole in the middle of the floor.

"There you are," he said. "That's the slippery-slip, sir – it goes round and round from top to bottom of the tree – and you fly out of a trapdoor at

163

the bottom, and land on a soft cushion of moss."

"Splendid!" said Santa Claus. "Will somebody else go first, please? Dear me – it's exactly the same as I read about in the books!"

"Er – I suppose you couldn't just change us back to our ordinary selves, could you?" asked Jo, afraid that in his excitement Santa Claus might forget to do what they so badly wanted. "I feel as if I'm going to somersault again, and I don't want to turn head-over-heels all the way down the slippery-slip."

"Change you back? Yes, of course; it's easy!" said Santa Claus. "The slippery-slip is just the right place for a spell. Shut your eyes, please."

They all shut their eyes. Santa Claus touched each one gently, chanting a curious little song:

"Go in as you are,
Come out as you were,
Go in as you are,
Come out as you were!"

They opened their eyes. Moon-Face got a cushion and pulled Bessie on to it. He gave her a tremendous push and she shot down the slippery-slip at top speed – round and round – and then out she flew through the trapdoor at the bottom, and landed on a tuft of moss.

"Oh!" she said, breathless. "Oh! I'm myself again. I'm not a stiff-jointed doll any longer – and I can shut and open my eyes properly!"

She got up – and out of the trapdoor flew Jo. "Jo! You're all right again! You're you!" cried Bessie in delight. "And here comes Silky – she's not a doll anymore – and here's Fanny – she's all right, too. Look out – here's the old Saucepan Man – hurrah he's back to normal!"

"And he's lost his floppy ears," said Silky. "I'm rather sorry. I liked him with those long ears. Good old Saucepan."

"And then, WhoooooOOOOOSH! The trapdoor shot open with a bang and out sailed Santa Claus, his hood on the back of his head! Bump! He went on to the cushion of moss, and sat there, panting and full of delight.

"What a thrill! WHAT a thrill! Better than anything I've got in my castle."

"Look out! Here comes Moon-Face!" cried Jo, and out came Moon-Face, no longer a fat teddy bear, but his own beaming self once more.

"I'd like to do that again," said Santa Claus, standing up. "How did you say we got back to the top of the tree? In a basket?"

"Yes," said Jo, "but if you don't mind, sir, we won't come with the others. You see, our mother will be wondering about us. So we'd better say good-bye and thank you very much."

"Good-bye. See you next Christmas," said Santa Claus. "I'll bring you something extra fine. Ah – here comes the basket, let down on a rope. Do we get in?"

The last thing that Jo, Bessie and Fanny saw was Santa Claus in the big basket, being pulled slowly up by all the squirrels at the top of the tree. Moon-Face and Silky and Saucepan were with him, leaning over the edge of the basket, waving to them.

"Well – I suppose dear old Santa Claus will be going down that slippery-slip till it's dark," said Jo. "Oh, dear – surely I'm not going to turn head-over-heels again! I feel just like it!"

"Oh, you'll soon get out of the habit," said Bessie. "I still feel as if I want to walk stiffly like a doll. I say – wasn't that an adventure!"

"We'll never have a better one," said Fanny.

Oh, yes, you will, Fanny, Bessie and Jo. You just wait and see!

XXVI

THE ARMY OF RED GOBLINS

One day Mother said that she would be out for the whole day, and, if the children liked, they could have the Old Saucepan Man to tea, and any other two friends they had made.

"Good!" said Jo. "We'll ask Moon-Face and Silky."

Bessie wrote a note, and gave it to the little white goat to take to Moon-Face.

The white goat was a wonderful creature. It gave the most delicious milk, it ran errands, and if any of the hens got out, it found them and drove them back. It was most useful.

The goat took the note in its mouth, and ran off to the Enchanted Wood. It came to the Faraway Tree and bleated to the red squirrel, who peeped out from his hole low down in the trunk.

The squirrel took the note and bounded up to Moon-Face with it. Moon-Face was delighted, and shouted down to Silky, who came up and read it.

"We'll ask the Old Saucepan Man as soon as Mister Watzisname is asleep," said Moon-Face. "The children haven't asked Watzisname — so Saucepan will have to creep down the tree with us, without telling him."

They sent a note back by the little goat, saying that they would arrive at three o'clock that afternoon. The children were excited. Mother had gone by that time, and the girls began to make the cottage look pretty with jars of flowers. Bessie baked some chocolate cakes, and Fanny made some toffee. Jo cut bread and butter.

"We'll have a fine tea," he said. "I hope the Saucepan Man won't be too deaf this afternoon."

By three o'clock everything was ready. The children were neat and clean. The table looked fine with its bread and butter, cakes, and toffee. Bessie went to the gate to look for their visitors.

She couldn't see them coming down the lane. "They *are* late!" she called to the others. "I expect the Saucepan Man has got tangled up with his saucepans or something!"

Half-past three came and no visitors. The children were rather disappointed. "Perhaps Moon-Face read my letter wrongly, and thought it was four o'clock," said Bessie.

But when four o'clock came and still no Moon-

Face, Silky, or Saucepan Man arrived, they got really worried.

"I do hope nothing has happened," said Bessie, feeling upset. "There's all our nice tea and nobody to eat it."

"We'll wait a bit longer, then we'll eat our share," said Jo. So, when five o'clock came, and nobody had arrived, the children sadly ate half the tea themselves.

"Something's happened," said Jo gloomily.

"Oh dear! What do you think it is?" said Bessie, alarmed. "Could we go and see?"

"No," said Jo. "Not now, anyway. Mother will be back soon. We'd better go to-night. The rope is let down the tree then for us to pull ourselves up by, and it won't take long to climb up."

"We really must find out what's wrong," said Bessie, clearing away. "We'll take their share of the tea with us."

So, that night, when it was quite dark, the three children slipped out of bed, dressed, and crept out of the back door. They had to take a lantern, for there was no moon that night. Jo swung it in front of him and they could see where to tread.

Down the dark lane they went, over the ditch and into the Enchanted Wood. The trees were whispering very loudly together to-night. "Wisha-wisha-wisha!" they said.

"Oh, how I wish I knew what they were saying!" said Fanny.

"Come on," said Jo. "We'd better not be too long, Fanny. We want to be back by daylight."

They made their way through the dark wood. As there was no moon there were no fairy-folk about at all that night. The children soon came to the Faraway Tree, and looked for the rope.

But there was no rope at all this time — and they had to begin to climb up as usual, holding on to the boughs carefully, for it was very difficult to see.

Before they had got farther than two branches up, a strange thing happened. Some one caught hold of Jo's shoulder and pushed him roughly down! Jo fell, caught hold of the lowest branch, and just saved himself in time.

"Who did that?" he cried angrily. He undid his lantern from his belt, where he had put it whilst climbing, and flashed it up the tree, calling to Bessie and Fanny to go no farther.

And standing grinning in the lower branches of the tree were four red goblins, with pointed ears, wide mouths, and wicked little eyes!

"No one is allowed to come up the tree now," said one of the goblins. "And no one is allowed to come down either."

"But why not?" asked Jo, astonished.

"Because it's *our* tree now!"

"*Your* tree! What nonsense!" said Jo. "We've come to see our friends who live in the tree. Let us pass."

"No!" said the goblins, and they grinned widely. "You — can't — come — up!"

"It's no good," said a tiny voice beside Jo. "The goblins have taken every one prisoner in the

169

tree. If you go up they'll only push you down, or take you prisoners too."

Jo flashed his lantern downwards, and the children saw that it was the little red squirrel speaking—the one who looked after the cushions for Moon-Face.

"Hallo!" said Jo. "Do tell me what's happened. I can't understand it!"

"Oh, it's easy enough to understand," said the squirrel. "The Land of the Red Goblins came to the top of the Faraway Tree. The goblins found the hole that leads down through the clouds, and poured down it! They took every one prisoner. Moon-Face and every one else are locked up in their houses in the tree-trunk. I can tell you Mister Watzisname and the Angry Pixie have nearly battered their doors down in rage!"

"But why have the goblins locked them up?" asked Bessie, in surprise.

"Well, they want some magic spells that the Tree-dwellers know," said the squirrel. "They are going to keep them all locked up till they tell the spells. Isn't it dreadful?"

"Oh dear!" said Fanny. "Whatever can we do to help them?"

"I don't know," said the squirrel sadly. "If only you could get up to them you might be able to make some plan. But the goblins won't let any one up the tree."

"Wisha-wisha-wisha-wisha!" whispered the trees loudly.

"You know, I can't help feeling that the trees

want to tell us something to-night," said Bessie suddenly. "I always feel that they are whispering secrets to one another — but to-night I feel that they want to tell them to *us!*"

"I shouldn't be surprised," said the squirrel. "The Faraway Tree is King of the Wood, and now that trouble has come to it all the other trees are angry. Perhaps they want to help us."

"Wisha-wisha-wisha," said the trees loudly.

"Put your arms round a tree-trunk and press your left ear to the tree," said the squirrel suddenly. "I have heard it said that that is the only way to hear a tree's words."

Each of the children found a small tree. They put their arms round the trunks and pressed their left ears to the trees. And then they could quite clearly hear what the trees were whispering.

"Help the Faraway Tree-dwellers!" the leaves whispered. "Help them!"

"But how can we?" whispered back the children eagerly. "Tell us!"

"Go up the slippery-slip," said the trees, in their leafy voices. "Go through the trap-door and up the slippery-slip!"

"Oh!" cried all the children at once. "Of course! Why ever didn't we think of it ourselves?"

"Sh!" said the squirrel, in alarm. "Don't let the goblins hear you. What did the trees say?"

"They said we were to go through the trap-door and up the slippery-slip," said Jo, in a low voice. "We can get right up to Moon-Face's then. It's a wonderful idea."

"Come on then!" said Bessie, and the three of them ran to the Faraway Tree, and felt about for the little trap-door. Ooooh! Another adventure!

XXVII

A MOST EXCITING NIGHT

"If only we can creep up the slippery-slip that runs right round and round the middle of the trunk, and get to Moon-Face's at the top, we shall be able to help him!" said Jo, feeling about for the trap-door.

"I wonder why Moon-Face didn't slip down it himself," said Bessie.

"Oh, he'd think that there would be plenty of red goblins at the bottom of the tree, ready to catch him when he flew out of the trap-door," said Jo. "But I don't believe they know about this slide!"

He found the trap-door and swung it open. "Hold it open for me whilst I climb in," he said. Bessie held it. Jo began to climb up.

But, dear me, it was most terribly slippery! He simply couldn't manage to get up the slippery-slip at all! As fast as he climbed up a little way he slid down again. He groaned.

"This is awful! We can never get up this way! I shall keep slipping down all the time."

"Let *me* try!" said Bessie eagerly. So Jo slid out of the trap-door and Bessie crept in. But it was just the same for her as for Jo. The slide was far too steep and slippery to be climbed.

"Wisha-wisha-wisha!" said the trees nearby. Bessie ran to one, put her arms round its trunk, and pressed her left ear to it. She listened.

"Tell the squirrel to go!" whispered the leaves. "Tell the squirrel to go!"

"Red squirrel, *you* go up!" said Bessie at once. "Can you manage to, do you think?"

"Yes," said the squirrel. "I have claws on my feet to hold with, and I am used to climbing. But what's the use of me going? I am not clever enough to make plans with Moon-Face."

"Wisha-wisha-wisha!" said the trees loudly. Jo pressed his ear to one. "The squirrel can throw a rope down the slippery-slip!" whispered the tree.

"Of course!" said Jo, in delight. "Why didn't I think of it?"

"Tell us," said the girls. Jo told them. "The squirrel must climb the slide to the top. He must ask Moon-Face for the rope that is let down for the cushions. But instead of letting it down through the branches of the tree, he must let it down through the slide inside. Then we can hang on and be pulled up!"

"Oooh! That's a really good idea," said Bessie.

"Sh!" said Jo, as he heard a shout from a goblin up the tree. "We don't want them to guess what we're doing."

"The goblins are coming down!" whispered Fanny in alarm. "I can hear them. What shall we do?"

173

"We'd better get inside the trap-door and sit at the bottom of the slippery-slip as quiet as mice," whispered Jo. "Go in first, squirrel, and climb up. You know what to do, don't you?"

"Yes," said the squirrel, and disappeared up the slide, digging his sharp little claws into it just as if he were climbing up the outside of a tree-trunk! Jo pushed Bessie inside and then Fanny. He climbed in himself and shut the trap-door just in time.

Three goblins jumped down to the foot of the tree and began hunting round about. "I *know* I heard some one!" said one of them.

"Well, so long as we don't let them pass us up the tree, they can't do much!" said another

with a laugh. "I don't think you heard any one
—it was just the trees whispering."

"Wisha-wisha-wisha!" said the trees at once.

"There! What did I tell you?" said the goblin.
They jumped back into the boughs of the Faraway Tree, and the children hugged one another
and chuckled.

"I wonder if the squirrel has got up to the top
of the slide yet," said Jo.

As he spoke a little sound came down the slide
—a soft, slinky sound—and something suddenly
touched them!

"Ooh! A snake!" cried Bessie in alarm.

"Don't be silly! It's the rope that the good
little squirrel has sent down!" said Jo, feeling it.
"Now, we'd better go up one at a time, for Moon-
Face will never be able to pull us all up at once."

Fanny went first. She was hauled all the way up
the slide. It was very strange, so dark and quiet.
At last she reached the top. Moon-Face was there,
red with pulling. A light burnt in his funny
round room. He was simply overjoyed to see
Fanny. He hugged her, and then sent down the
rope for Bessie. She came up—and then Jo.

"Don't make too much noise," said Moon-
Face in a low voice, as he squeezed them all.
"The goblins are outside every one's door."

"Oh, Moon-Face, we're so sorry you are captured like this," said Jo. "Couldn't you have
slid down the slide and escaped? Or did you think
there might be goblins at the bottom?"

"Well, I did," said Moon-Face, "but I also

175

thought that if I slid down I'd be leaving all my friends behind in the tree, and that seemed a mean thing to do."

"Yes, it would be rather mean," said Jo, "to save yourself and leave the others. Moon-Face, what can we do to help?"

"Well, I simply don't know," said Moon-Face. "I've thought and I've thought—but I can't think of anything really good at all."

"It's a pity Silky isn't here," said Jo. "We could talk it all over with her then. She's clever."

"We can't possibly get at *her*," said Moon-Face. "She's locked in, just as I am."

"Jo! Moon-Face!" said Fanny suddenly, her face red with excitement. "I've thought of a way to help."

"What?" cried the others.

"Well—couldn't the red squirrel slip down the slide, out of the trap-door, and take a note to the brownies in the wood?" asked Fanny. "Do you remember how we helped them when we first came to the wood—they said they would always be pleased to help us if we wanted them?"

"Yes,—but how could *they* help?" asked Moon-Face doubtfully. Nobody quite knew. But Jo suddenly nodded his head and gave a squeal.

"Sh!" said every one at once

"Sorry," said Jo, "but I really have got an idea at last. Listen! The red squirrel can tell the brownies to come up here in crowds—we'll pull them up on the rope. Then Moon-Face can shout out to the goblins outside that he'll tell them the magic spells they want to know — and when they open the door the brownies and ourselves can all pour out and defeat the goblins!"

"That's a *splendid* idea!" said Moon-Face, looking at Jo in admiration.

"Simply wonderful!" said the girls. Jo was pleased.

"And we'll unlock every one's doors and they can all join in!" he said. "My word, this is going to be exciting! Can you see how dreadfully angry the Angry Pixie will be — and Mister Watzisname? My goodness, they'll go for the red goblins like wild cats!"

Every one chuckled. The red squirrel touched Jo's knee. "Will you give me the note then?" he said. "I know where Mister Whiskers lives, and I will take the letter to him, and let him call all the brownies together."

Jo took out his pencil and wrote a note on Moon-Face's paper. He folded it and gave it to the red squirrel, who folded it even smaller and tucked it inside his cheek.

"That's in case I'm caught by the goblins," he said. "They'll never think of looking for a note inside my cheek!" He sat on his bushy tail, gave himself a push, and set off down the slippery-slip at a tremendous pace.

Fanny giggled. "His tail is a cushion," she said. "Isn't he a darling? I do hope he'll find Mister Whiskers all right."

"Well, we'd better just sit quietly and wait," said Moon-Face. "I don't want the goblins opening my door and seeing you all here. They'll know we've got a plan then."

"We brought you the tea you didn't eat this afternoon," said Bessie, and she undid the bag. "Here are some radish sandwiches, some buns, and some toffee."

"We'll all have some," said Moon-Face. "And I've got some Pop Biscuits too."

So they sat round quietly on Moon-Face's curved sofa and bed and chairs, and ate and whispered, waiting for the squirrel to come back with Mister Whiskers and the brownies. Whatever would happen then?

XXVIII

THE RED GOBLINS GET A SHOCK

It seemed a long time before anything happened. Then Moon-Face pricked up his ears and listened. "Some one's coming up the slippery-slip," he said. "It must be the little squirrel."

"I hope it isn't a goblin!" said Fanny, looking rather scared.

But it was the red squirrel. He hopped out of the slippery-slip hole and nodded at every one. "It's all right," he said. "The brownies are coming. I found Mister Whiskers and he has slipped out to fetch all his family. There are fifty-one of them!"

"We'd better let down the rope then," said Moon-Face, and he let it slither down the slide. Some one caught hold of it at the other end, and the rope tightened.

"There's a brownie there now!" said Moon-Face, and he and Jo hauled on the rope. It was heavy. They pulled and they pulled, panting hard.

"This brownie is jolly heavy!" said Jo. And no wonder—for when they at last got the rope to the top, there was not one brownie—but five, hanging on to the rope! They leapt into Moon-Face's tiny round room, and began to whisper excitedly. Moon-Face told them all about the goblins, and they grinned when they heard his plan.

Down went the rope again, and this time six brownies came up on it. By this time the room was very crowded. But nobody minded.

"We'll have to sit on each other's knees," said Jo, and giggled at the sight of so many people in Moon-Face's little tree-room.

The brownies all looked exactly the same. They all had very long beards, though Mister Whiskers' beard was the longest. It reached right down to his toes.

The rope fetched up all the fifty-one little men, and by that time there was really no room to move! Every one was excited, and there was such a lot of whispering that it sounded like a thousand leaves rustling at once!

"Now I'm going to bang on the inside of my door and tell the goblins I will let them know the magic spell they want!" said Moon-Face. "As soon as they open the door you must all pour out and either push them down the tree or take them prisoner."

"I say, I've thought of such a good idea," said Jo suddenly. "Let's push them all into this room of Moon-Face's—and send some one down the tree to bolt the trap-door—then when they slide down, thinking to escape, they'll all be nicely boxed up in the slide till we open the trap-door and let them out! Then we can take them one by one and tie them up!"

"That *is* a good idea," said Mister Whiskers. "Two brownies had better go up the ladder that leads through the clouds, to stop any goblins trying to escape that way—and six of us had better slide down to the foot to stop them escaping into the wood."

Six of the brownies at once took cushions and slid down the slippery-slip. They shot out of the trap-door, and bolted it on the outside. They surrounded the foot of the tree, ready to prevent any goblins from escaping.

The rest of them waited for Moon-Face to speak to the goblins outside. They were all tremendously excited.

Moon-Face banged on the inside of his door. A goblin outside shouted to him:

"Stop that noise!"

"Let me out!" yelled Moon-Face.

"Not till you tell us any magic spell you know!" said the goblin.

"I know a spell that will turn people into kings and queens!" shouted Moon-Face.

"Tell us it then," said the goblin at once.

"Well, open my door," said Moon-Face. There came the sound of a key turned in a padlock, and then Moon-Face's door was opened. At once the whole crowd of brownies poured out like a stream of water! Jo, Bessie, and Fanny went out with them, and when the goblins saw the crowd, they gave a yell and leapt down the tree to warn their friends.

Two brownies leapt up to the ladder and sat there to prevent any goblins from escaping to the land above. Jo, Moon-Face, Bessie, and Fanny climbed quickly down the tree to let out all the people locked into their homes. How glad every one was!

Mother Washalot was very angry at being locked in. "I'll teach those goblins to lock me in!" she shouted. And the old dame picked up her washtub and began to throw the water over all the goblins climbing about the tree. What a shock for them! Jo couldn't help laughing.

He unlocked Mister Watzisname's door, and out came Watzisname, shouting and raging, followed by the Saucepan Man. Watzisname seemed to be all fists, and he flew at the goblins and began to pommel them as if he were beating carpets!

The Saucepan Man acted in a surprising manner. He took off one saucepan after another, one kettle after another, and threw them at the escaping goblins. Crash! Bang! Clatter! My goodness, he was a good shot! Fanny stopped and watched him in amazement.

They let out the Barn Owl, and the three owls that lived together. They flew at the goblins, screeching and hooting. The Angry Pixie was so very angry that he flew at Jo when he let him out, and Jo only just explained in time that he must fight the goblins and not him, Jo.

Bessie let Silky out, but Silky was frightened by all the noise and shouting. Still she managed to catch one goblin by tying him up with one of her curtains. Silky and Bessie then took the goblin up the tree and pushed him into Moon-Face's room. When he found the slippery-slip he slid down it in delight, thinking he could escape. But, alas for him, he stopped at the bolted trap-door, and there he stayed, unable to climb up or to get out!

Many other goblins were caught that way too. They tried to escape from the brownies by running down the tree to the wood—but when they found six strong brownies at the foot they climbed up the tree again to escape into their own land at the top! And then, of course, they found two brownies on the ladder, who pushed them down again.

So into Moon-Face's house they went, hustled there by Jo, who took a great delight in pushing them in. One by one they tried to escape by sliding down the slippery-slip, and soon the slide was crowded with goblins, piled one on top of the other!

Dawn came, and the sun shone out, lighting

up the great branches of the enormous Faraway Tree.

"Now we can see if any goblins are hiding anywhere," called Moon-Face, who was thoroughly enjoying himself. So he and the brownies and Watzisname looked into every hole and corner, behind every branch and tuft of leaves, and pulled out the hidden goblins there. They were marched up to Moon-Face's room and pushed down the slippery-slip. Soon there wasn't a single goblin left. They were all piled on top of one another in the slide, most uncomfortable and frightened.

"There!" said Moon-Face at last, pleased with himself and every one else. "We've got them all safe. My word, I *am* hungry! What about having a good meal?"

"Look!" called Silky, waving to a lower part of the great tree. "The Faraway Tree is growing ripe plums just down there! What about having a feast of those?"

"Good!" said Moon-Face. "Squirrel, go down to the six brownies at the foot of the tree and tell them they can come up now. Hi, you two brownies on the ladder, you can come down. Silky, can you make some cocoa to drink? Plums and cocoa would make a lovely meal."

Just as they were sitting down to eat and drink, a strange figure came up the tree. He was thin and ragged and knobbly, but his face beamed as if he knew everybody.

"Who's that?" said Fanny at once.

"Don't know," said Moon-Face, staring.

"I seem to have seen his face before," said Bessie.

"He's a funny-looking creature," said Jo. "He looks rather like a scarecrow to me!"

The ragged man came up, and sat down on a branch nearby. He held out his hand for a cup of cocoa.

"Who are you?" said Moon-Face.

"What's your name?" asked Silky.

"Play a game?" said the thin man, beaming. "Yes, certainly—what game shall we play?" And then every one knew who it was! It was the Old Saucepan Man—without his kettles and saucepans! He had thrown them all at the goblins, and now he had none left to wear.

"Saucepan! You *do* look different!" said Watzisname, hugging him. "I didn't know you! Come and have a plum."

The Saucepan Man looked alarmed. "Hurt your *thumb*?" he said. "Oh, I *am* sorry!"

"No, I didn't say I'd hurt my thumb," said Watzisname, roaring with laughter, and clapping Saucepan on the back. "I said, have a *plum*, a *plum*, a *plum*!"

"Thanks," said the Saucepan Man, and put two large plums into his mouth at once.

"And now," said Moon-Face, when every one had finished, "what about those goblins in the slippery-slip?"

184

XXIX

THE PUNISHMENT OF THE RED GOBLINS

"It's certainly time we dealt with those red goblins," said Mister Whiskers, the chief brownie, wiping his long beard with a yellow handkerchief. He had dropped plum-juice all down it.

And just at that moment there came a great surprise. A deep voice behind them said "Oho! Here's a nice little company! What about coming back with me into Wizard Land and doing a few jobs?"

Every one turned in dismay. They saw a curious figure above them, leaning down from a big branch. It was a wizard, whose green eyes blinked lazily like a cat's.

"It's Mighty-One the Wizard!" said Moon-Face, and he got up to bow, for Mighty-One was as mighty as his name. Every one did the same.

"Who is he?" whispered Fanny.

"He's the most powerful wizard in the whole world," whispered back Silky. "He's come down the ladder — so that means that the Land of Red Goblins has gone and the Land of the Wizards has come! They are always on the look-out for servants, and I suppose Mighty-One has come down to look for some."

"Well, I'm not going to be servant to a wizard," said Fanny.

"You won't be," said Silky. "He's not a bad fellow. He won't take any one who doesn't want to go. It's good training for a fairy who wants to learn magic."

Mighty-One blinked his eyes slowly and looked at the little crowd on the branches before him. "I need about a hundred servants to take back with me," he said. "Who will come?"

Nobody said a word. Moon-Face got up and bowed again.

"Your Highness," he said, "we none of us want to leave the Enchanted Wood, where we are very happy. You may perhaps find others who would like to go back with you. We beg you not to take any of us."

"Well," said the wizard, sliding his green eyes from one person to another, "I haven't much time. My land will swing away from the Far-away Tree in about an hour. Can you get me the servants I want? If you can, I will not take you."

Everybody looked worried. But Jo jumped up with a beaming face.

"Your Highness! Would red goblins do for your servants?"

"Excellently," said Mighty-One. "They are quick and obedient—but goblins would never agree to coming with me! They belong to their own land."

Moon-Face, Watzisname, and the Saucepan Man all began to talk at once. Mighty-One lifted up his hand and they stopped. "One at a time," said the wizard.

So Moon-Face spoke. "Sir," he said, "we have about a hundred goblins boxed up in the middle of this tree. They tried to take us prisoner. It would be a very good punishment for them if we gave them to you to take away to your land as servants."

Mighty-One looked astonished. "A hundred goblins!" he said. "That is very strange. Explain."

So Moon-Face explained. Mighty-One was most interested to hear of the fight.

"We'll all go down to the bottom of the tree and let the goblins out one by one," said Jo, excited. "Come on! What a shock for them when they see the wizard!"

So they all trooped down the tree in the bright rays of the rising sun. Really, it was all most exciting!

They came to the trap-door at the foot of the tree. Behind it they could hear a lot of shouting and quarrelling and pushing.

"Don't push!"

"You're squashing me!"

Moon-Face unbolted the trap-door and opened it. Out shot a red goblin and fell on a green cushion of moss. He picked himself up, blinked in the bright sunlight, and then turned to run. But Mighty-One tapped him with his wand and he stood still. He couldn't move! He looked scared when he saw the wizard.

One by one the red goblins tumbled out of the trap-door, and were tapped by the wizard. Ten, twenty, thirty, forty, fifty, sixty — they came shooting out of the trap-door, surprised and frightened, sliding gradually down the slippery-slip, as one after another slid from the trap-door.

Fanny giggled. It was a funny sight to see.

"It's a very good punishment for those bad goblins," she said to Silky. "They came down the ladder to trap *you* and now some one else has trapped *them*, and is taking them back to his land!"

The red goblins stood in a sulky row, quite unable to run away. "Quick — *march*!" said the wizard, when the last one had slid out of the trap-door — and up the tree went the sulky goblins. It was no use trying to escape. The wizard had put a spell into their legs, and they had to go up to the top of the tree, through the big white cloud and into Wizard Land.

"A jolly good riddance of bad rubbish," said Jo. "My word, what an exciting night we've had! I *did* enjoy it."

"Isn't it cold!" said the Saucepan Man, shivering.

"Cold!" cried Bessie and Fanny, who were feeling hot in the morning sun. "Why, it's as warm as can be."

"It's because he hasn't got his kettles and saucepans hung round him as usual," said Watzisname. "I expect they feel like a coat to him. Poor old Saucepan!"

"I don't like the look of him without his saucepans," said Fanny. "He doesn't look right. Can't we collect them for him? They're on the ground — and all about the tree."

So they began to collect the Saucepan Man's belongings. He was very pleased. They hung his kettles on him, and put his saucepans all round him, with his special one for a hat. Some of them were dented and bent, but he didn't mind a bit.

"There!" said Fanny, pleased. "You look like yourself now. You looked horrid without all your saucepans on — like a snail without its shell."

"I never had a bell," said the Saucepan Man.

"SHELL, I said," said Fanny.

"Smell?" said the Saucepan Man, looking round. "I can't smell anything at the moment. What sort of smell — nice or nasty?"

"*Shell*, not smell," said Fanny patiently.

"Oh, *shell*. What shell?" said the Saucepan Man. But Fanny had forgotten what she had said, and she shook her head and laughed. "Never mind!" she shouted.

"We really must go," said Jo. "Mother will be up and wondering whatever has happened to us. Oh dear—I do feel sleepy! Come on, girls."

They said good-bye to all the tree-dwellers and set off through the Enchanted Wood. Silky went back to her house in the tree, wondering what had happened to her clock, which hadn't joined in the fight at all. It had been fast asleep.

Moon-Face went back to the tree, yawning. Watzisname and the Saucepan Man climbed back, so tired that they fell fast asleep before they reached their hole, and had to be put safely in the corner of a broad branch by the Angry Pixie, in case they fell down.

Dame Washalot went back, making up her mind to do no washing *that* day. Soon there was peace in the tree, and only the snores of Watzisname could be heard.

Far away up the tree in the Land of the Wizards the red goblins were working hard. Ah—they had got a good punishment, hadn't they? They wouldn't be in such a hurry to catch other people in future.

The three children got home, and their mother stared at them in surprise.

"You *are* up early this morning," she said. "I thought you were still in bed and asleep.

190

Fancy getting up and going out for a walk before breakfast like that."

How sleepy the children were that day! And, dear me, didn't they go to bed early that night!

"No more wandering through the Enchanted Wood and up the Faraway Tree for me to-night," said Jo, as he got into bed. "I vote we don't go there for a long time. It's getting just a bit too exciting."

But it wasn't long before they went again, as you will see!

XXX

A PLAN FOR BESSIE'S BIRTHDAY

A week later it was Bessie's birthday. She was very excited, because Mother said she might have a little party.

"We'll ask all our friends in the Faraway Tree," she said.

"Do you think we'd better?" said Jo doubtfully. "I don't think Mother would like Dame Washalot —or Mister Whiskers—or the Angry Pixie."

"Well, we can't very well ask some and not others," said Bessie. "The ones we left out would be very hurt indeed."

"It's awkward," said Fanny. "We'd better go and tell Moon-Face and Silky, and ask them what to do."

But Mother wouldn't let the two girls go off

191

with Jo that day. She said there was a lot of iron-
ing to do, and they must help.

"Oh, bother!" said Fanny to Jo. "You'll have
to go alone, Jo, and ask Moon-Face and Silky
what we ought to do about our party. Don't be
too long, or we'll be worried about you. And
please don't go climbing up into any strange land
without us."

"Don't worry!" said Jo. "I'm not going to visit
any more lands at the top of the Faraway Tree.
I've had enough adventures to last me for the rest
of my life!"

He set off. He ran through the Enchanted Wood
and came to the Faraway Tree. It was a hot afternoon and not many little folk were about.

It seemed almost too hot to climb the tree. Jo
whistled. The little red squirrel popped down from
the tree and looked at him.

"Leap up to the top of the tree and ask old
Moon-Face if he'll drop me down a rope with a
cushion on the end, and haul me up, squirrel,"
said Jo.

The squirrel bounded lightly up the tree. Soon
a rope, with a cushion tied to it, came slipping
down the tree. Jo caught hold of it. He sat
astride on the cushion and tugged the rope. It
began to go up the tree, bumping into branches
as it went.

It was a funny ride, but Jo enjoyed it. He waved
to the Angry Pixie, who was sitting outside his
house. He stared at Jo in surprise and then
grinned when he saw who it was. The owls

were all asleep in their homes. Mister Watzisname was awake for once, and fell out of his chair in alarm when he suddenly saw Jo swinging up through the air, bumping into boughs!

When he saw it was Jo, he was so pleased that he fell off his branch on to the Saucepan Man, who was snoozing in a chair just below.

"Oooooch!" said the Saucepan Man, startled. "What's the matter? What are you jumping on me for?"

"I'm not," said Watzisname. "Look, there's Jo!"

"Go? I don't want to go," said the Saucepan Man, settling down again. "Don't be so restless."

"I said, 'There's JO!'" roared Watzisname.

"Where?" said the Saucepan Man in surprise, looking all round. But by that time, of course, Jo was far away up the tree, laughing over funny Watzisname and dear old Saucepan!

Watzisname climbed back to his chair and shut his eyes. Soon his snores reached Jo, who was far above, hoping that Silky would see him and go up to Moon-Face's to talk to him. He forgot to look out for Dame Washalot's water, but it missed him nicely, splashing down heavily on to poor old Watzisname, making him dream that he was falling out of a boat into the sea.

Silky did see him, and waved. She climbed the tree quickly to go up to Moon-Face's. By the time she got there Jo had just arrived and was getting off the cushion.

"Hallo!" said Moon-Face and Silky, pleased

to see him. "Where are Bessie and Fanny?"

Jo told them. He told them about Bessie's birthday too, and her difficulty about how many people she should ask.

"We'd like every one," said Jo. "But Mother wouldn't like some of them, we are sure. What shall we do?"

"I know! I know!" said Silky, clapping her hands suddenly. "Next week the Land of Birthdays comes to the top of the Faraway Tree—and any one who has a birthday can go there and give the most wonderful party to all their friends. Oh, it would be lovely! Last time the Birthday Land came, nobody had a birthday, so we couldn't go. But this time we can, because Bessie could ask us all!"

"It sounds good," said Jo. "But I didn't really want to go into any strange land again, you know. We always seem to get mixed up in queer adventures. So far we've always escaped all right—but we might not another time."

"Oh, no harm can come to you in the Land of Birthdays!" said Moon-Face, at once. "It's a wonderful land. You really *must* come! It's a chance you mustn't miss."

"All right," said Jo, beginning to feel excited. "I'll tell the girls when I go back."

"And we'll tell every one in the tree, and Mister Whiskers. and his brownies too," said Silky. "Bessie would like every one to go, wouldn't she?"

"Oh yes!" said Jo. "What happens, though? I

mean, do we have to arrange about tea, or anything? And what about a birthday cake? Fanny was going to make one for Bessie."

"Tell her not to," said Silky. "She'll find everything she wants up in the Birthday Land. My word, we *are* lucky! Fancy some one really having a birthday just as the Birthday Land comes along!"

"Bessie's birthday is on Wednesday," said Jo. "So we'll go up the tree then. I'd better go back and tell the girls now. I said I wouldn't be long."

"Have a Toffee Shock?" said Moon-Face.

"No, thank you," said Jo. "I'd rather have a Pop Biscuit."

So they sat and munched the lovely Pop Biscuits, and talked about the exciting time they had had with the red goblins.

"Now I really must go," said Jo, and he got up. He chose a red cushion, said good-bye to Silky and Moon-Face, and shot off down the slippery-slip. Jo thought he really could do that all day, it was such a lovely feeling! He flew out of the trap-door at the bottom and landed on the moss. He got up and ran off home.

The girls were pleased to see him back so soon. When they heard about the Birthday Land they were tremendously excited.

"Ooooh!" said Bessie, going red with joy. "I *am* lucky! I wonder what will happen. Do you suppose there will be a cake for me?"

"Rather!" said Jo. "And lots of other things too, I expect!"

195

"We shall have to tell Mother," said Fanny. "I wonder if she will let us go."

Mother didn't seem to mind. "I expect it's just some sort of birthday joke your friends in the wood are playing on you!" she said. "Yes, you can go, if you like. Our cottage is really too small for a very large party."

"I shall wear my best dress," said Bessie happily. "The one Mother got me last week, with the blue sash!"

But Mother wouldn't let her!

"No," she said firmly. "You will all go in your old clothes. I remember quite well what you looked like when you went off to tea with that funny friend of yours, the Old Saucepan Man. I certainly shall not allow any of you to wear nice things next Wednesday."

Bessie was nearly in tears. "But, Mother, I can't go to my own birthday party in old clothes," she said.

But it was no good. Mother said they could wear old clothes or else not go. So there was no help for it.

"I don't know what every one will think of us, going to the Birthday Land in our oldest things," said Jo gloomily. "I've a good mind not to go."

But when Wednesday afternoon came, they all thought differently! Old clothes or not, they meant to go!

"Come on!" said Jo. "It's time we went to the Land of Birthdays!"

XXXI

THE LAND OF BIRTHDAYS

The children set off once again to the Enchanted Wood. They knew the way to the Faraway Tree very well by now.

"Wisha-wisha-wisha!" whispered the trees, as the children ran between them. Bessie put her arms round one, and pressed her left ear to the trunk. "What secret are you saying to-day?" she asked.

"We wish you a happy birthday," whispered the leaves. Bessie laughed! It was fun to have a birthday!

When they came to the Faraway Tree, how marvellous it looked! The folk of the tree had decked it with flags because it was Bessie's birthday, and it looked simply lovely.

"Ooooh!" said Bessie, pleased. "I do feel happy. The only thing I wish is that I had proper party clothes on, not my old ones."

But that couldn't be helped. They were just about to begin to climb the tree when Dame Washalot's big washing-basket came bumping down on the end of Moon-Face's rope for the children to get into.

"Good," said Jo. "Get in, girls." They all got in and went up the tree at a tremendous rate. "Moon-Face must have some one helping him to pull," said Jo, astonished.

He had. Mister Whiskers was there, with

Watzisname and the Old Saucepan Man, and they were all pulling like anything. No wonder that basket shot up the tree!

"Many happy returns of the day," said every one, kissing Bessie.

"Oh, good! You're not in your best clothes," said Moon-Face. "We wondered if you would make it a fancy-dress party, Bessie."

"Oh, I'd love to!" said Bessie. "But we haven't got any fancy dresses."

"We can easily get those in the Birthday Land!" said Silky, clapping her hands for joy. "Good, good, good! I do like a fancy-dress party."

"Everybody is ready to go," said Moon-Face. "The brownies are just below us. Where's Saucepan? Hie, Saucepan, where have you got to?"

"He stepped into your slippery-slip by mistake," said a brownie, appearing out of Moon-Face's house. "He went down the slide with an awful noise. I expect he's at the bottom by now."

"Good gracious! Just like silly old Saucepan!" said Moon-Face. "We'd better let down the washing-basket for him, or he'll never get up to us!"

So down went the basket again, and old Saucepan got into it and came up with a clatter of saucepans and kettles.

"Now are we really all ready?" said Moon-Face. "Silky—Watzisname—Saucepan—the Angry Pixie—Dame Washalot—Mister Whiskers—the brownies . . ."

"Gracious! What a lovely lot of people are coming!" said Bessie, seeing all the brownies and

198

tree-folk on the branches below. "Is that Mother Washalot? What a nice old woman!"

Dame Washalot was fat and beaming. For once n a way she was going to leave her wash-tub. Going to the Land of Birthdays was not a treat to be missed!

"Come on, then," said Moon-Face, and he led the way to the ladder. Up he went, popped his head above to make quite sure that the Land of Birthdays was there, and then jumped straight into it!

Every one climbed up. "That's all, I think," said Moon-Face, peering down. "Oh no—there's some one else. Whoever is it? I thought we were all here?"

"Gracious! It's my clock!" said Silky. "The one I got in the Land of Take-What-You-Want!"

Sure enough, it was. "Ding-dong-ding-dong!" it cried indignantly, as it climbed up on its flat feet.

"All right, all right, we'll wait for you!" said Silky. "Go carefully up the ladder. You weren't really asked, you know."

"Oh, I'd love your clock to come to my party," said Bessie at once. "Come along, clock."

"Ding-dong," said the clock, pleased, and managed to get up the ladder.

The Land of Birthdays was simply beautiful. To begin with, there was always birthday weather there—brilliant sunshine, blue sky, and a nice little breeze. The trees were always green, and there were always daisies and buttercups growing in the fields.

"Oh, it's lovely, it's lovely!" cried Bessie, dancing round joyfully. "Moon-Face, what about fancy dresses? Where do we get them?"

"Oh, you'll find them in that house over there," said Moon-Face, pointing to a very pretty house. They all trooped over to it. As they went, small brown rabbits hopped out of holes, called "A Happy Birthday!" to Bessie, and popped back. It was all very exciting.

Every one crowded into the pretty house. It was full of cupboards—and in the cupboards were the most thrilling dresses you can think of.

"Oh, look at this!" cried Jo, in delight, as he came across a Red Indian's dress, with a wonderful head-dress of bright feathers. "Just the right size for me!"

He put it on. Bessie chose a dress like a fairy's, and Fanny chose a clown's dress with a pointed hat. She looked fine.

Moon-Face dressed up as a pirate and Silky became a daffodil. Watzisname was a policeman, and as for the Old Saucepan Man, he simply could *not* find a fancy dress to fit him, because he was so bumpy with kettles and saucepans!

Every one else dressed up and, dear me, they did look fine! Bessie had wings with her dress, but she was disappointed because she couldn't fly with them. How she would have loved to spread them and fly, as the real fairies did!

"Now for balloons!" said Silky, and she danced into the sunshine and ran to an old balloon woman who was sitting surrounded by a great cloud of coloured balloons. Everybody chose one, and what games they had!

Suddenly a tea-bell rang, and Moon-Face gave a scream of joy.

"Tea! Birthday tea! Come on, every one!"

He rushed to a long, long table set out in the field. Bessie ran with the others, and took her place at the head. But to her great surprise and disappointment there was no food on the table at all — only just empty plates, cups, and glasses!

"Don't look so upset!" whispered Silky. "You've got to wish your own tea!"

Bessie gave a squeak. Wish her own tea! Oooh! That would be the best fun in the world!

"Don't wish for bread-and-butter!" called Moon-Face. "Wish for orange jelly. I like that!"

"I wish for orange jelly!" said Bessie at once. And immediately a large, fat wobbly orange jelly appeared on one of the empty dishes. Moon-Face helped himself.

"Wish for strawberries and cream!" cried Fanny, who simply loved those.

"I wish for strawberries and cream!" said Bessie, and an enormous dish of strawberries appeared, with a large jug of cream beside it. "And I wish for chocolate biscuits too — and iced lemonade — and chocolate blancmange — and treacle pudding — and strawberry ices — and — and — and . . ."

"Fruit salad!" yelled some one.

"Sausage rolls!" cried Watzisname.

"Jam tarts!" begged Mister Whiskers.

"Ding-dong-ding-dong!" said Silky's clock in the greatest excitement. Every one laughed.

"Don't wish for ding-dongs!" said Jo. "We've got plenty of those, as long as Silky's clock is here!"

The clock struck fourteen without stopping. It wandered about, looking as happy as could be.

Every one began to eat. My goodness, it was a wonderful tea! The strawberries and cream and the ices went almost at once, for Mister Whiskers and fifty brownies liked those very much. So Bessie had to wish for some more.

"What about my birthday cake?" she asked Silky. "Do I wish for that too?"

"No. It just comes," said Silky. "It will appear right in the middle of the table. You just watch."

Bessie watched. There was a wonderful silver dish in the middle of the table. Something seemed to be forming there. A curious sort of mist hung over it.

"The birthday cake is coming!" shouted Jo, and every one watched the silver dish. Gradually a great cake shaped itself there—oh, a wonderful cake, with red, pink, white, and yellow icing. All round the side were flowers made of sweets. On the top were eight candles burning, for Bessie was eight that day. Her name was written in big sugar letters on the top: "BESSIE. A VERY HAPPY BIRTHDAY!"

Bessie felt very proud. She had to cut the cake, of course. It was quite a difficult job, for there were so many people to cut it for.

"This is a wishing-cake!" said Moon-Face, when every one had a piece on their plate. "So wish, wish, wish, when you eat it—and your wish will come true!"

The children stared at him in delight. What should they wish? Fanny was just holding her cake in her hand, thinking of a wish, when the Old Saucepan Man upset everything! Whatever do you think he did?

XXXII

THE LITTLE LOST ISLAND

"Wouldn't you like to wish?" said Moon-Face, turning to the Old Saucepan Man, who was just about to bite his cake.

"Fish?" said the Saucepan Man, in delight. "Yes, I'd love to fish! I wish we were all fishing for fine fat fishes in the middle of the sea."

Well! What a wish to make, just as he was eating a wishing-cake! Of course, Saucepan didn't know it was a wishing-cake, for he hadn't heard Moon-Face properly.

Anyway, the wish immediately came true. A wind blew down, and lifted up the whole crowd of guests at the table. Sitting on their chairs, clinging tightly, they flew through the air for miles!

Whatever was happening?

Down flew the chairs in the big wind. A shower of salt spray drenched every one. Jo gasped and looked down. Bump! He and every one else landed on soft sand, rolled off their chairs, and sat up, blinking in surprise.

The long-bearded brownies looked frightened. Moon-Face kept opening and shutting his mouth like a fish, he was so astonished. Jo was cross, and so was the Angry Pixie.

"*Now* what's happened?" said Dame Washalot, in a most annoyed voice. "Why have we come here?"

"Look at all those fishing-rods!" said Silky, pointing to a whole row of rods standing in the sand, with their lines in the water.

"Waiting for *us*!" groaned Moon-Face. "Silly old Saucepan didn't hear what I said about wishing — he thought I said *fishing* — and he wished us all here, fishing in the sea!"

"Goodness!" said Bessie, alarmed. "Where are we, then?"

"I think we're on the Little Lost Island," said Silky, looking round. "It's a funny little place, always floating about and getting lost. But there's always good fishing to be had from it."

"Fishing!" said Jo, in disgust. "Who wants to go fishing in the middle of a birthday party? Let's get back at once."

"Ding-dong-ding-dong!" said Silky's clock, walking about at the edge of the sea and getting its feet wet in the waves.

"Come back, clock!" called Silky. "You know you can't swim."

The clock came back and wiped its wet feet on the grass that grew around. Bessie thought it was a remarkably sensible clock, and she wished she had one like it. "I say, you know, we really must do something about getting back to the Land of Birthdays," said Jo, getting up and looking round the little island. "What can we do? Is there a boat here?"

There was nothing except the fishing-rods! Nobody took up even one of those, for they didn't feel in the least like fishing. The Little Lost

Island was just a hilly stretch of green grass and nothing else whatever.

"I really don't know *what* to do!" said Moon-Face, frowning. "Do you, Mister Whiskers?"

Mister Whiskers was dressed up like Santa Claus, and looked very fine indeed, with his long beard. He rubbed his nose thoughtfully and shook his head.

"The difficulty is," he said, "that none of us has any magic with him, because we're all in fancy dress and our other clothes are in the Land of Birthdays. So the spells and magic we keep in our pockets are not here."

"Well, we shan't starve," said Watzisname. "We can always fish."

"Fancy eating fish and nothing but fish always!" said Jo, making a face. "When I think of all those lovely things that Bessie wished for — and nobody to eat them now! Really, I could cry!"

Fanny had something in her hand and she looked down to see what it was. It was a piece of the birthday cake. Good! She could eat that, at any rate. She lifted the delicious cake to her mouth and took a nibble.

"What are you eating?" asked Moon-Face, bending over to see.

"A bit of the birthday cake," said Fanny, cramming all of it into her mouth.

"Don't eat it! Don't swallow it!" yelled Moon-Face suddenly, dancing round Fanny as if he had gone mad. "Stop! Don't swallow!"

Fanny stared at him in astonishment. So did every one else.

"What's gone wrong with Moon-Face?" asked Silky anxiously. Fanny stood still with her mouth full of birthday cake, looking with amazement at Moon-Face.

"What's the matter?" she asked, with her mouth full.

"You've got a bit of the wishing-cake in your mouth, Fanny!" shouted Moon-Face, hopping first on one leg and then on the other. "Wish, you silly girl, wish!"

"What shall I wish?" said Fanny.

"Wish us back in the Land of Birthdays, of course!" yelled every one in excitement.

"Oh," said Fanny, "I didn't think of that! I wish we were all back in the Land of Birthdays, eating our tea!"

Darkness fell round every one very suddenly. No wind came this time. Moon-Face put out his hand and took Silky's. What was happening?

Then daylight came back again — and every one gave a shout of surprise and delight. They were back in the Land of Birthdays! Yes — there was the table in front of them and more chairs to sit down on, and the same delicious food as before!

"Oh, good, good, good!" shouted every one, and sat down at once. They beamed at one another, very thankful to be back from the Little Lost Island.

"What a queer little adventure!" said Jo, helping himself to a large piece of wishing-cake. "Please be careful what you wish, everybody—we don't want any more adventures like that in the middle of a party!"

"I wish that my wings could fly!" said Bessie, as she munched her cake. And at once her silver wings spread themselves out, and she rose into the air like a big butterfly, flying beautifully. Oh, it was the loveliest feeling in the world!

"Look at me—look at me!" she cried—and every one looked. Fanny called out to her. "Don't fly too far, Bessie. Don't fly too far!"

Bessie soon flew down to the table again, her cheeks red with excitement and joy. This was the loveliest birthday party she had ever had!

Everybody wished their wishes except the Old Saucepan Man, who had already wasted his. Fanny, too, had wished her wish when she was on the Little Lost Island, but when she looked upset because she had lost her wish, Moon-Face whispered to her.

"Don't be upset. Tell me what you really wanted to wish and I'll wish it for you. I don't want a wish for myself."

"Oh, Moon-Face, you *are* kind!" said Fanny. "Well, if you really mean it, I did want a doll that could walk and talk."

"Easy!" said Moon-Face at once. "I wish that Fanny had a doll that walks and talks."

And at that very moment Silky cried out in wonder and pointed behind her. Every one looked. Coming along on small, plump legs was a doll, beautifully dressed in blue, with a bag in its hand.

It walked to Fanny and looked up at her.

"Oh! You lovely, beautiful doll!" cried Fanny in the greatest delight, and she lifted the doll on to her knee. It cuddled up to her and said, "I belong to you. I am your own doll. My name is Peronel."

"What a sweet name!" said Fanny, hugging the doll. "What have you got in that bag, Peronel?"

"All my other clothes," said the doll, and opened her bag. Inside were nightdresses, a dressing-gown, an overcoat, a mackintosh, overalls, dresses, and all kinds of other clothes. Fanny was simply delighted.

"What did you wish, Jo?" asked Bessie. Jo was looking all round and about as if he expected something to arrive at any moment.

"I wished for a pony of my own," said Jo. "Oh! Look! Here it comes! What a beauty!"

A little black pony, with a white mark on its forehead and four white feet, came trotting up to the party. It went straight to Jo.

"My own pony!" cried the little boy, in delight. "Let me ride you! I shall call you Blackie."

He jumped on the pony's back and together they went galloping round the Land of Birthdays.

"Now let's play games!" cried Moon-Face, capering about. And as soon as he said that, the tea-table vanished and music began to play.

"Musical chairs! Musical chairs!" shouted Silky, as the chairs suddenly put themselves together in a long row. "Come on, everybody!"

SAFE BACK HOME AGAIN—
AND GOOD-BYE!

The party went on and on. The game of Musical Chairs was fun, for instead of somebody taking away a chair each time, the end chair took itself away, walked neatly off, and stood watching.

Silky won that game. She was so quick and light on her feet. A big box of chocolates came flying down through the air to her, when she sat down on the very last chair and pushed Moon-Face away! She was delighted.

"Let's all have one!" she said, and undid the box at once. Whilst they were eating they saw a most astonishing sight.

"Look!" said Moon-Face, almost swallowing his chocolate in astonishment. "What's this coming?"

Every one looked. It seemed like a lot of little brightly coloured men, running very upright. What do you suppose they were?

"Crackers!" shouted Watzisname, jumping off his seat in delight. "Crackers—running to us— ready to be pulled!"

Really, those crackers were the greatest fun! They ran about on tiny legs, dodging away, trying not to be caught! Every one ran after them, laughing and shouting. One by one the gay crackers were captured, and then they were pulled. My goodness, what glorious things there were inside!

"I've got a golliwog brooch!" cried Fanny, pinning it on herself.

"I want one too," said her doll.

"Well, you must catch a cracker then, Peronel," said Fanny, and how she laughed to see her doll running about after a red cracker! Peronel caught one at last and brought it back to Fanny. Inside there was a teddy-bear brooch, which Peronel was simply delighted with!

Jo found a silver whistle in his cracker. It whistled like a blackbird. Jo was very proud of it. Moon-Face found a squeaker that squeaked like a cat mewing, and made the Old Saucepan Man go hunting for cats all the time! Naughty Moon-Face! He pressed his squeaker behind the Saucepan Man and laughed till he cried to hear him calling, "Puss! Puss! Puss!" and looking under tables and chairs.

Silky's clock wanted a cracker too. So it ran after one, and trod on one to catch it. It held it with its foot and pulled it with Silky. What do you suppose was in it? A tiny tin of polish with a duster wrapped round it!

"Just the thing to clean you with!" said Silky in delight. The clock was very pleased. It struck twenty-two times without stopping, much to the walking doll's astonishment.

They played hide-and-seek, and immediately the most exciting bushes and trees sprang up everywhere to hide behind. Really, the Birthday

Land was the most exciting country to be in!

Then they played "Here we come gathering nuts and may," and two big nut trees grew behind them full of nuts, and a long hedge white with sweet-scented may. It made the game seem very real.

When they played "Here we go round the mulberry bush," a big mulberry tree grew up as they danced, and the children gave a shriek of delight and picked the ripe red mulberries to eat. You never knew what was going to happen next, but you might be sure it was something exciting!

Then they thought they would have races—and, hey presto! they saw a crowd of small motor-cars running up, all ready to be raced! In got every one, choosing the car they liked best. There was even a tiny one for Peronel the doll, and an extra one for Silky's clock, who joined in the fun and ding-donged merrily all the time.

The Old Saucepan Man won the race, though he dropped a few saucepans on the way. Moon-Face handed him a box of sweets that had appeared for the winner.

"You've won!" he said.

"Run?" said the Saucepan Man. "All right, I'll run!" And he ran and ran, just to show how fast he could run when he wanted to. What a noise he made, with his kettles and saucepans clattering all round him!

"Supper-time, supper-time!" shouted Moon-Face suddenly, and he pointed to a lovely sight. About a hundred toadstools had suddenly grown up, and appearing on them were jugs of all kinds of delicious drinks, and cakes and jellies and fruit. Smaller toadstools grew beside the big ones.

"They are for seats!" cried Silky, sitting down on one and helping herself to some acornade. "I'm hungry! Come on, every one!"

Bessie flew down from the air. She did so love flying. Fanny ran up with her doll, who followed her everywhere, talking in her little high voice. Jo galloped up on his pony. Every one was very happy.

It began to get dark, but nobody minded, because big lanterns suddenly shone out every-where in the trees and bushes. As they sat and ate, there came a loud bang-bang-bang!

Peronel cuddled up to Fanny, frightened. Silky's clock tried to get on to Silky's knee, scared, but she pushed it off.

"What's that?" said Jo, patting his frightened pony.

"Fireworks! Fireworks!" shouted the Angry Pixie in delight. "Look! Look!"

And there, in front of them, were the fireworks, setting themselves off beautifully. Rockets flew high and sizzled down in coloured stars. Catherine-wheels whizzed round and round. Squibs jumped and banged. Golden feathers poured down like fountains. Really, it was glorious to watch!

"This is the loveliest birthday party I've ever heard of," said Bessie happily, flapping her big wings, as she sat and watched the fireworks. "Lovely things to eat—wishes that come true—most exciting games—glorious crackers—and now fireworks!"

"We have to go home at midnight," said Moon-Face, pushing away Silky's clock, which was trying to sit on his toadstool with him.

"How shall we know when it's midnight?" asked Fanny, thinking that really it was quite time her doll went to bed.

They knew all right—because when midnight came Silky's clock stood up straight and struck loudly, twelve times—Dong-dong-dong-dong-dong-dong-dong-dong-dong-dong-dong-dong!

"To the ladder! To the ladder!" cried Moon-Face, hurrying every one there. "The Birthday Land will soon be on the move!"

The ladder was there. Every one climbed down it and called good-bye. The brownies took cushions and slid off down the slippery-slip. Mister Whiskers got his beard caught round the legs of Moon-Face's sofa and nearly took that with him down the slide. Moon-Face just stopped it in time, and unwound his beard.

"What about my pony?" asked Jo anxiously. "Do you suppose he will mind sliding down, Moon-Face?"

"Well, he can't climb down the tree, and he certainly wouldn't like going down in the washing-basket," said Moon-Face. So they sat the surprised pony on a cushion and he slid down in the greatest astonishment, wondering what in the world was happening to him!

Fanny slid down with her sleepy doll on her knee. Bessie carefully took off her wings and folded them up. She didn't mean to have them spoilt. She wanted to use them every day. She was very proud of them.

The pony arrived on the cushion of moss quite safely. Jo mounted him. It was dark in the wood, but the moon was just rising, and they would be able to see their way home quite well.

"Good-bye!" called Moon-Face from the top of the tree. "We've had a lovely time!"

"Good-bye!" called Silky. "Ding-dong!" said her clock sleepily.

"Take care of yourselves!" shouted Watzisname.

Moon-Face pressed his squeaker loudly, and then giggled to hear the Saucepan Man call,

215

"Puss, Puss, Puss! Wherever *is* that cat!"

Slishy-sloshy-slishy-sloshy! Good gracious, was Dame Washalot doing washing already? Jo dodged away on his pony and the girls ran from the tree. Mister Whiskers got the water all over him, for he was standing near by, and he was most disgusted.

"Come on, girls!" said Jo, laughing. "We really *must* go home! We shall never wake up in the morning!"

So they went home once more, through the Enchanted Wood, with the moon shining pale and cold between the trees.

"Wisha-wisha-wisha!" whispered the leaves.

Jo put his pony into the field outside the cottage. Fanny undressed Peronel and put her into her dolls' bed. Bessie put her wings carefully into a drawer. They all undressed and got sleepily into bed.

"Good-night!" they said. "What a lovely day it's been. We *are* lucky to live near the Enchanted Wood!"

They were, weren't they? Perhaps they will have more adventures one day; but now we must say good-bye to them, and leave them fast asleep, dreaming of the Land of Birthdays, and all the lovely things that happened there!

Enid Blyton

THE FOLK OF THE FARAWAY TREE

Jo, Bessie and Fanny are fed up when they hear that Connie is coming to stay – she's so stuck-up and bossy. But they don't let her stop them having exciting adventures with their friends Silky, the elf; Moon-Face and the Saucepan Man.

Together they climb through the cloud at the top of the tree and visit all sorts of strange places, like the Land of Secrets and the Land of Treats – and Connie learns to behave herself!

You can share more adventures of the Faraway Tree in

The Magic Faraway Tree

Enid Blyton

THE MAGIC FARAWAY TREE

"Oh, do let's take our lunch up into the Land of Topsy-Turvy. Oh, do, do!"

Dick thought it would be dull in the country with Jo, Bessie and Fanny. But that was before he found the magic Faraway Tree! The four children have the most extraordinary adventures with the Saucepan Man, Moon-Face and Silky the elf. They only have to climb through the cloud at the top of the huge tree to be in the Land of Spells, or Land of Topsy-Turvy, or even the Land of Do-As-You-Please!

Jo, Bessie and Fanny go on more
exciting escapades in

The Folk of the Faraway Tree

Enid Blyton

THE SAUCY JANE FAMILY

"Welcome to the Saucy Jane!"

Mike, Belinda and Ann spend their holidays on a beautiful houseboat on the canal – and what an exciting time they have! They learn to swim and have some wonderful holiday treats – like taking a trip on a real canal boat.

Enid Blyton

THE SEASIDE FAMILY

They were off – off to Sea-gull Cove by the sea!

Mike, Belinda and Ann are going on a seaside holiday. What's more, they are taking their home with them – it's easy when you live in a caravan! And what a wonderful summer lies ahead, with the sea right outside their door!